TRANZLATY

Language is for everyone

اللعه للجميع

The Call of Cthulhu

نداء كيولو

H.P. Lovecraft

إتش. بي. لافكرافت

English

العربيه

www.tranzlaty.com

The Horror Made of Clay
الرعب المصنوع من الطين

There is one thing I find particularly merciful.

هناك سيء واحد أجده رحيماً بسكل حاص.

The inability of the human mind to correlate events.

عدم قدره العقل البسري على ربط الاحداث ببعصها.

It's a blessing that we can't understand the world.

إنها نعمه أنا لا نسطيع فهم العالم.

We live blissfully on a placid island of ignorance.

نعيس فن سعاده عامره على جريره هادنه من الجهل.

An island in the midst of black seas of infinity.

جريره وسط بحار سوداء لا مساهيه.

And it was not meant that we should voyage far.

ولم يكن المقصود أن سافر بعيداً.

The sciences each strain in their own directions.

نجه كل العلوم فن انجاهابها الحاصه.

But hitherto science's findings have harmed us little.

لكن حنى الآن لم نصرنا نانج العلم إلا قليلا.

But some day dissociated knowledge will be pieced
together.

لكن فن يوم من الأيام سيم نجميع المعرفه المنفرقه.

Terrifying vistas of reality will open up to us.

سنفسح أمامنا آفاق مرعبه من الواقع.

And we will be left in a frightful vantage point.

وسنرك فن موقف مرعب.

We will either go mad from the revelation we are given.

إما أنا سنصاب بالجنون من جراء هذا الكسف الذى سنلقاه.

Or we will flee from the deadly light that we will see.

أو سهرب من النور القانل الذى سنراه.

We will run from the knowledge we had always pursued.

سهرب من المعرفه النى كنا نسعى إليها دائماً.

And we will seek the peace and safety of a new dark age.

وسسعى إلى السلام والأمان فن عصر ظلام جديد.

Theosophists have guessed at the scale of the cosmos.
لقد حمن أباع البوصوفيه حجم الكون.

Our world is but a transient incident in this cycle.
عالما ليس سوى حادنه عابره فن هده الدوره.

The human race plays but a little role in the universe.
لا يلعب الجس البسرى سوى دور صيل فن الكون.

The theosophists have hinted at strange methods of survival.
ألمح أباع البوصوفيه إلى أساليب غريبه للبقاء على قيد الحياه.

But their suggestions would freeze a rational man's blood.
لكن اقتراحاتهم كفيله بتجميد دم أى رجل عاقل.

Only the optimism of their ideas hides the horror.
إن تفاول أفكارهم وحده هو ما يخفن الرعب.

But it is not their ideas that chill me the most.
لكن أفكارهم ليس هن ما يبير قسعريره فن جسدى أكثر من غيرها.

It is something else that fills me with terror.
هناك سىء آخر يملأنن بالرعب.

The single glimpse of forbidden eons I have seen.
لمحه واحده من عصور محرمه رأيتها.

When I think of what I saw my blood stands still.
عندما أفكر فيما رأيته، يتوقف دمن عن النبض.

Restlessness plagues my dreams since that glimpse.
مند تلك اللمحه، باتت أحلامن تعانن من الارق والقلق.

It came to me like all dreaded glimpses of truth.
لقد أتت إلن كما لو كانت لمحات مخيفه من الحقيقه.

An accidental piecing together of separated things.
بتجميع غير مقصود لاسياء منفصله.

An old newspaper item and the notes of a dead professor.
مقال صحفن قديم وملاحظات أساد متوفى.

In a flash everything was pieced together before me.
فن لحظه، اتصحت لن الصوره كامله.

I hope no one else will accomplish this terrible insight.

ألمى ألا يحمق أي سحص آحر هده الرويه المروعه.

Certainly, if I live, I shall never help anyone to know it.
بالمأكيد، إدا عست، فلن أساعد أحداً على معرفه دلك.

I shall never knowingly supply a link in so hideous a chain.
لن أساهم عن علم أبداً فى إنراء هده السلسله البسعه.

I think that the professor, too, intended to keep silent.
أعمقد أن الاساد أيضاً كان يبوى البرام الصمت.

He didn't mean to share the secrets that he knew.
لم يكن يمصد أن يمسى الاسرار التى كان يعرفها.

And I'm sure he would have destroyed his notes.
وأنا مسأكد من أنه كان سيدمر ملاحطابه.

If he had not been seized by sudden and suspicious death.
لو لم يكن قد لقن حسفه فجأه وبسكل مريب.

***

My knowledge of the thing began in the winter of 1926-27.
بدأت معرفتى بهدا الامر فى ساء عام 1926-1927.

My great-uncle was the professor George Gammell Angell.
كان عمى الاكبر هو البروفيسور جورج جاميل أنجيل.

He was the Professor Emeritus of Semitic languages.
كان أسادأ فحرياً للعات الساميه.

He lectured in Brown University, Providence, Rhode Island.
ألقى محاصرات فى جامعه براون، بروفيدس، رود آيلاند.

His death, at the age of ninety-two, triggered the event.
أدى موبه، عن عمر يباهر 92 عاما، إلى وقوع هذا الحدت.

He was widely known as an authority on ancient inscriptions.
كان معروفاً على نطاق واسع بأنه مرجع فى المووس القديمه.

Heads of prominent museums came to him for his expertise.
كان روساء المساحف البارره يأنون إليه للاسعاده من حبربه.

So his death was noticed by many within academic circles.

لذا فقد لاحظ الكثيرون فى الأوساط الأكاديميه وفاته.

Interest was intensified by the obscurity of his death.

وقد ازداد الاهتمام بسبب غموص وفاته.

It occurred as he was disembarking from the Newport boat.

حدث ذلك أثناء نزوله من قارب نيوبورت.

Witnesses say a dark nautical-looking fellow had jostled him.

ويقول الشهود إن رجلاً داكن البشره ذو مظهر بحرى قد دفعه.

After being stricken, he fell suddenly, witnesses say.

ويقول شهود عيان إنه سقط فجاه بعد إصابته.

Physicians were unable to find any visible disorder.

لم يتمكن الاطباء من العثور على أى اصطراب ظاهر.

After some perplexed debate they reached their conclusion.

وبعد نقاس محير، توصلوا إلى استنتاجهم.

"It must have been a lesion of the heart," they agreed.

واتفقوا قائلين: "لا بد أنه كان جرحاً فى القلب."

"After all, he was rather an elderly man," they added.

وأضافوا: "على أى حال، كان رجلا مسنا نوعاً ما."

"the brisk ascent of the steep hill caused his end."

"كان الصعود السريع للتله شديده الانحدار سبباً فى نهايته."

At the time I saw no reason to dissent from this dictum.

فى ذلك الوقت لم أر أى سبب لمعارضه هذا القول.

But latterly I am inclined to wonder about their conclusion.

لكنى موخراً أميل إلى التساول عن استنتاجهم.

And I do more than just wonder if they were right.

وأنا لا أتساءل فقط عما إذا كانوا على حق.

***

My grand-uncle died alone as a childless widower.

توفى عمى الاكبر وحيداً كأرمل بلا أبناء.

And so I became heir and executor to his possessions.

وهكذا أصبح الوريث والمعد لوصيه على مملكانه.

So I was expected to go over his papers and writings.
لذلك كان من المتوقع أن أراجع أوراقه وكتاباته.

I moved his entire set of files and boxes to my Boston home.
نقلت جميع ملفاته وصناديقه إلى منزلي في بوسطن.

Much of the materials I collected will later be published.
سيتم نشر معظم المواد التي جمعتها لاحقاً.

Many academics in his field took great interest in his work.
أبدى العديد من الاكاديميين في مجاله اهتماماً كبيراً بعمله.

The American archeological society relied on him greatly.
اعتمدت عليه الجمعيه الاثريه الامريكيه بشكل كبير.

But there was one box which I found exceedingly puzzling.
لكن كان هناك صندوق واحد وجدته محيراً للغايه.

I felt much averse from showing these files to other eyes.
شعرت بنفور شديد من عرض هذه الملفات على الاخرين.

The box had been locked, unlike the other boxes.
كان الصندوق مغلقاً، على عكس الصناديق الاخرى.

And initially I found no key that would open this box.
وفي البدايه لم أجد مفتاحاً يفتح هذا الصندوق.

But then the location of the key occurred to me.
لكن بعد ذلك خطر لي فكره مكان المفتاح.

The professor always carried a keyring in his pocket.
كان الاستاد يحمل دائماً سلسله مفاتيح في جيبه.

It was indeed one of these keys that opened the box.
كان أحد هذه المفاتيح هو الدى فتح الصندوق بالفعل.

But in the box was a still more closely locked barrier.
لكن داخل الصندوق كان هناك حاجز أكثر إحكاماً.

What could be the meaning of the queer bas-relief?
ما هو المعنى المحتمل لهذا النحس البارز الغريب؟

Various paper cuttings accompanied the bas-relief.
يصحب النقوش البارزه قصاصات ورقيه متنوعه.

What did the disjointed jottings and ramblings allude to?

إلى ماذا كانت تشير تلك الحربسات والترتراب المقطعه؟

Had my uncle become credulous to superficial impostures?

هل أصبح عمي ساذجاً يصدق عمليات الاحتيال السطحيه؟

Perhaps in his later years his criticalness thought slowed.

ربما في سنواته الاخيره تراجعت حده تفكيره النقدى.

Someone had disturbed this old man's peace of mind.

لقد أزعج أحدهم راحه بال هذا الرجل العجوز.

And so I resolved to locate the eccentric sculptor.

وهكذا عزمت على العثور على النحات غريب الاطوار.

The man who set in motion my uncle's strange obsession.

الرجل الذى أشعل شراره هوس عمي الغريب.

***

The bas-relief was roughly shaped like a rectangle.

كان النقش البارز على شكل مستطيل تقريبا.

The rectangular shape was less than an inch thick.

كان الشكل المستطيل أقل سمكا من بوصه واحده.

And the bas-relief was about five by six inches in area.

وكانت مساحه النقش البارز حوالى خمسه في سته بوصات.

It was obvious that the bas-relief was of modern origin.

كان من الواضح أن النقش البارز ذو أصل حديث.

The designs, however, were far from modern in atmosphere.

لكن التصاميم كانت بعيده كل البعد عن الطابع العصرى.

The inscriptions suggested a far older civilization.

تشير النقوش إلى حضاره أقدم بكثير.

The vagaries of cubism and futurism were many and wild.

كانت تقلبات التكعيبيه والمستقبليه كثيره وجامحه.

But normally such patterns fail to produce regularity.

لكن عاده ما تفشل هذه الانماط في إنتاج انتظام.

The cryptic regularity which lurks in prehistoric writing.

الانتظام الغامض الكامن في الكتابه ما قبل التاريخ.

This regularity was certainly present in the bas-relief.

كان هذا الانطام موجودا بالتأكيد فن النقس البارر.

I was certain the inscriptions represented a writing system.

كنت متأكداً من أن النقوس تمثل نطام كتابه.

I had some familiarity with the papers of my uncle.

كانت لدئ بعض المعرفه بأوراق عمى.

And I had looked through all of his collections and works.

وقد اطلعت على جميع مجموعاته وأعماله.

But I failed to find any writing that was similar.

لكن لم أجد أئ كتابه مماتله.

I could not geographically place this alphabet in any way.

لم أسطع تحديد موقع هذه الابجديه جعرافياً بأى سكل من الاسكال.

Nor could I guess from what time this writing came from.

ولا أسطيع أن أحمن من أئ رمن كتب هذه الكتابه.

Above these apparent hieroglyphics there was a figure.

وفوق هذه النقوس الهيروعليميه الطاهره كان هناك سكل.

The figure was evidently only of pictorial intent.

كان من الواصح أن السكل كان دا عرص نصويرى فقط.

The impressionism of the picture added to the mystery.

أصفى الطابع الانطباعى للصوره مزيداً من الغموص.

No clear idea of the creature's nature could be discerned.

لم يكن من الممكن اسسفاف أئ فكره واصحه عن طبيعه المحلوق.

The creature seemed to be a monster, of some sort.

بدا المحلوق وكأنه وحس من نوع ما.

Or the symbol represented a monster, of some sort.

أو ربما كان الرمر يمثل وحساً من نوع ما.

Only a diseased mind could conceive of such a form.

لا يمكن أن يتصور مثل هذا السكل إلا عقل مريص.

My imagination yielded different pictures simultaneously.

أبدعت محيلتى صوراً محتلفه فى آن واحد.

But my imagination may also be somewhat extravagant.

لكن ربما يكون حيالى مفرطاً بعص السىء.

An octopus, a dragon, and also a human caricature.

أحطبوط، وبيس، ورسم كاريكاتورى لإنسان.

I shall try not be unfaithful to the spirit of the thing.
سأحاول ألا أكون غير مخلص لروح الامر.

A pulpy, tentacled head surmounted a scaly body.
رأس دو لب كيف ومحالب يعلو جسداً معطى بالحراسف.

Rudimentary wings protruded from the grotesque shape.
بربز أجنحه بدائيه من الشكل العريب.

But the shape of the monster wasn't even the worst part.
لكن سكل الوحس لم يكن حتى الجزء الاسوأ.

The background of the picture was even more frightening.
كانت حلفيه الصوره أكثر رعباً.

The scenery had a vague suggestion of another civilization.
كان للمناطر الطبيعيه إيحاء عامض بوجود حضاره أخرى.

Cyclopean architecture from a forgotten part of the world.
عماره عملاقه من منطقه منسيه من العالم.

***

Only some notes and press cuttings accompanied the oddity.
لم يرافق هذا السيء الغريب سوى بعض الملاحطات وقصاصات الصحف.

The press cuttings seemed to be only vaguely related.
بدت قصاصات الصحف دات صله عامصه فقط.

The hand written notes were all from my uncle.
كانت جميع الملاحطات المكتوبه بخط اليد من عمى.

But his notes made no pretense to any literary style.
لكن ملاحطاته لم تتطاهر بأى أسلوب أدبى.

There was no ordering mechanism to any of the papers.
لم يكن هناك آليه لترتيب أى من الاوراق.

Although there seemed to be a master document to the
notes.
على الرغم من أنه يبدو أن هناك وثيقه رئيسيه للملاحطات.

This document was ascribed to the cult of Cthulhu

نُسِب هذه الوئيمة إلى عباده كـولو

The word's letters had been painstakingly written out.

لقد كُتِب حروف الكلمه بعنايه فائمه.

There should be no erroneous reading of the unheard of word.

لا يبعتي أن يكون هناك قراءه حاطئه للكلمه غير المسموعه.

This Cthulhu manuscript was divided into two sections;

تم تقسيم مخطوطه كاثولو هذه إلى قسمين؛

The first manuscript was titled the following:

كان عنوان المخطوطه الاولى كما يلي:

"1925 - Dream and Dream Work of H. A. Wilcox"

"1925 - حلم وعمل الاحلام لهـ. أ. ويلكوكس"

"7 Thomas St., Providence, Road Island"

"7 سارع توماس، بروفيدس، رود آيلاند"

And the second manuscript was titled the following:

أما المخطوطه الثانيه فكان عنوانها كالتالي:

"Narrative of Inspector John R. Legrasse"

"سرد المفتس جون ر. ليغراس"

"121 Bienville St., New Orleans, 1908 Meetings."

"121 سارع بيانفيل، نيو أورليانز، اجتماعات عام 1908".

"Notes on Same, & Prof. Webb's account of events"

"ملاحظات حول سام، وروايه البروفيسور ويب للاحداث"

The other manuscript papers were all brief notes.

أما أوراق المخطوطه الاخرى فكانت جميعها عباره عن ملاحظات موجزه.

Some manuscripts described the queer dreams of different persons.

وصف بعض المخطوطات أحلامًا غريبه لأشخاص مختلفين.

Some manuscripts cited from theosophical books and magazines.

بعض المخطوطات المذكوره مأخوذه من كتب ومجلات ثيوصوفيه.

Notably, most of these citations were from W. Scott-Eliott.

والجدير بالذكر أن معظم هذه الاستشهادات كانت من دبليو سكوت إليوت.

Mainly the notes referenced Atlantis and the Lost Lemuria.

أسارت الملاحظات بسكل رئيسى إلى أطلانس وليوموريا المفقوده.

The other notes commented on long-surviving secret societies.

أما الملاحظات الأخرى فقد علقت على الجمعيات السريه التى استمرت لفتره طويله.

Hidden cults that may or may not still exist somewhere.

طوائف سريه قد تكون موجوده فى مكان ما أو لا.

Two books seemed to provide most of the information;

يبدو أن كتابين قد وفرا معظم المعلومات؛

Miss Murray's Witch-Cult in Western Europe.

طائفه الساحره الآنسه موراى فى أوروبا العربيه.

This book thoroughly detailed Mythological sources.

هذا الكتاب يفصل مصادر الاساطير بسكل سامل.

And Frazer's Golden Bough provided anthropological sources.

وقدم كتاب "الغصن الذهبى" لفريزر مصادر أنثروبولوجيه.

***

The cuttings largely alluded to outré mental illnesses.

أسارت المقاطع بسكل كبير إلى أمراض عقليه غريبه.

Outbreaks of group folly and mania in the spring of 1925.

نفسى حالات من الحماقه والهوس الجماعى فى ربيع عام 1925.

The first half of the manuscript told a very peculiar tale.

يحكى النصف الاول من المخطوطه قصه غريبه للغايه.

1925, the 1st of March, a thin dark young man came to my uncle.

فى الأول من مارس عام 1925، جاء ساب نحيف أسمر البسره إلى عمى.

The manuscript describes his neurotic and excited aspect.

بصف المخطوطه جانبه العصبى والمتحمس.

And he bore with him the strange bas-relief.

وحمل معه النفس البارز الغريب.

At that time the bas-relief was exceedingly damp and fresh.
فى دلك الوقت، كان النقس البارد رطباً وجديداً للغايه.

His card bore the name of Henry Anthony Wilcox.
كانت بطاقته تحمل اسم هنرى أنتونى ويلكوكس.

And my uncle had slightly recognized who he was.
وقد تعرف عمى عليه قليلا.

He was the youngest son of an excellent family.
كان الابن الأصغر لعائله ممتازه.

Latterly he had been studying sculpture at Rhode Island.
كان يدرس النحت فى رود آيلاند مؤخراً.

He lived alone at the Fleur-de-Lys Building.
كان يعيش وحيداً فى مبنى زهره الزنبق.

His residences were near the university.
كانت مساكنه قريبه من الجامعه.

Wilcox was a precocious youth of known genius.
كان ويلكوكس شابا موهوبا يتمتع بعبقريه معروفه.

But he was also known for his great eccentricity.
لكنه كان معروفاً أيضاً بغرابته الشديده.

From childhood he had excited the attention of others.
كان يثير انتباه الاخرين منذ طفولته.

He told of strange stories no one had told him about.
روى قصصاً غريبه لم يخبره بها أحد من قبل.

And he was in the habit of relating strange dreams.
وكان معتاداً على سرد أحلام غريبه.

He described himself as "psychically hypersensitive".
وصف نفسه بأنه "شديد الحساسيه النفسيه."

But those around him had other descriptions for him.
لكن من حوله كانت لديهم أوصاف أخرى له.

They were staid folk of the ancient commercial city.
كانوا أناسا رصينين من المدينه التجاريه القديمه.

And they dismissed him as merely strange and "queer".
وقد رفضوه ووصفوه بأنه مجرد شخص غريب و"شاد."

And so he never mingled much with his kind.

ولذلك لم يحلط كيراً بأماله.

And he had dropped gradually from social visibility.

وقد تراجع ظهوره الاجتماعن تدريجياً.

Now he is known only to a small group of esthetes.

أما الآن، فهو معروف فقط لمجموعه صغيره من دوئ الدوق الرفيع.

And those who knew him came mostly from other towns.

أما الدين عرفوه فكانوا فن العالب من مدن أخرى.

Even the Providence art club had found him quite hopeless.

حتى نادى بروفيدس للفنون وجده ميووساً منه نماماً.

Of course they were anxious to preserve their conservatism.

وبالطبع كانوا حريصين على الحفاظ على محافظتهم.

***

The professor's manuscript continued to describe the visit.

وواصل محطوطه الاسناد وصف الزياره.

The sculptor abruptly asked for his host's archeological knowledge.

سأل النحات فجأة مضيمه عن معرفته بعلم الآثار.

He wanted him to identify the hieroglyphics on the bas-relief.

أراد منه أن يتعرف على الهيروغليفيه الموجوده على النفس البارز.

He spoke in a dreamy and rather stilted manner.

تحدث بأسلوب حالم ومتكلف إلى حد ما.

His speech suggested pose and alienated sympathy.

كان حطابه يوحن بالتطاهر وينفر العاطف.

And my uncle showed some sharpness in his reply.

وأظهر عمن بعض الحده فن رده.

Because the bas-relief was still conspicuously freshness.

لأن النفس البارز كان لا يزال يعكس نضاره واصحه.

So there was no need for any kinship with archeology.

لذلك لم نكن هناك حاجه لاى صله قرابه بعلم الآثار.

Young Wilcox's rejoinder was of a fantastically poetic cast.

كان رد الساب ويلكوكس دا طابع سعرى رابع.

My uncle must have been impressed with the reply.

لا بد أن عمى قد أعجب بالرد.

And he recorded the reply of Wilcox verbatim.

وسجل رد ويلكوكس حرفياً.

"The bas-relief is indeed still conspicuously fresh."

"إن النقس البارر لا يرال يبدو جديداً بسكل واصح".

"Because I made this bas-relief last night, after a dream."

"لأسن صنعت هذا النقس البارر الليله الماصيه، بعد حلم".

"A dream of strange cities and stranger people."

"حلم بمدن غريبه وأناس أغرب".

"And dreams are older than brooding Tyros."

"والأحلام أقدم من نيروس الكئيب".

"Dreams are older than the contemplative Sphinx."

"الأحلام أقدم من نمال أبو الهول المتأمل".

"And dreams are older than the garden-girdled Babylon."

"والأحلام أقدم من بابل المحاطه بالحدائق".

This type of speech turned out to be characteristic of him.

اتصح أن هذا النوع من الكلام كان سمه مميزه له.

It was then that he began that rambling tale.

عندها بدأ يروى تلك الحكايه المسعبه.

The tale which suddenly played upon a sleeping memory.

الحكايه التى عادت فجأه إلى دكرى نائمه.

The tale that won the fevered interest of my uncle.

القصه التى أثارت اهتمام عمى السديد.

***

There had been a slight earthquake tremor the night before.

وقد حدثت هزه أرضيه طفيفه فى الليله السابقه.

The most considerable tremor New England had felt for some years.

كانت هذه أقوى هزه أرضيه سعرت بها نيو إنجلاند منذ سنوات.

Wilcox's imagination had been keenly affected by the earthquake.

لقد تأثرت مخيله ويلكوكس بشده بالزلزال.

He had had an unprecedented dream of great Cyclopean cities.

كان لديه حلم غير مسبوق بمدن عملاقه ضخمه.

He dreamed of Titan blocks and sky-flung monoliths.

كان يحلم بكتل تيتان وصخور ضخمه معلقه فى السماء.

All the architecture was dripping with green ooze.

كانت جميع المبانى مغطاه بسائل أخضر لزج.

And his dreams were sinister with latent horror.

وكانت أحلامه مسمومه تنم عن رعب كامن.

Hieroglyphics had covered the walls and pillars.

كانت الكتابه الهيروغليفيه تغطى الجدران والأعمده.

From somewhere underneath there came a sound.

صدر صوت من مكان ما فى الأسفل.

The sound was of a voice, but it was not a voice.

كان الصوت يشبه صوتاً، لكنه لم يكن صوتاً.

A chaotic sensation which only fancy could transmute into sound.

إحساس فوضوى لا يمكن تحويله إلى صوت إلا من خلال الخيال.

He attempted to say the almost unpronounceable word.

حاول أن ينطق الكلمه التى يصعب نطقها.

A jumble of unlikely letters; "Cthulhu fhtagn",

مجموعه من الحروف غير المتوقعه؛كثولولو فوحتاغن

This verbal jumble was the key to my uncle's recollection.

كان هذا التداخل اللفظى هو المفتاح لذاكره عمى.

This strange sound excited and disturbed Professor Angell.

أثار هذا الصوت الغريب حماسه البروفيسور أنجيل وأزعجه.

He questioned the sculptor with scientific minuteness.

اسجوب النحاب بدقه علميه مساهيه.

He studied the bas-relief with almost frantic intensity.
درس النقس البارر بكثافه سبه محمومه.

My uncle blamed his old age, Wilcox afterward said.
قال ويلكوكس لاحقاً إن عمي أرجع السبب إلى كبر سه.

In his younger days he would have recognized the hieroglyphics.
فى سبابه كان سيعرف على الكتابه الهيروغليفيه.

The pictorial design wouldn't have puzzled his sharper mind.
لم يكن التصميم التصويرى ليحير عقله الحاد.

Many of his questions seemed highly out of place to his visitor.
بدت العديد من أسئله عريبه للعايه بالنسبه لرائره.

He tried to connect him to strange mythological cults.
حاول ربطه بطوائف أسطوريه عريبه.

He tried to get him to admit affiliation to secret societies.
حاول أن يجعله يعترف بانسمانه إلى جمعيات سريه.

My uncle even promised to keep his visitor's secret.
بل إن عمي وعد بالحفاظ على سر رائره.

"Are you not part of a widespread mystical group?"
"ألست جزءا من جماعه صوفيه واسعه الانسار؟"

"Are you not a member of a paganly religious body?"
"ألست عصواً فى هيئه ديىيه وسيه؟"

Eventually he became convinced the sculptor wasn't a member.
وفى النهايه اقتنع بأن النحاب لم يكن عصواً.

He was indeed ignorant of any cult or system of cryptic lore.
كان جاهلا بالفعل بأى طائفه أو نطام من المعارف العامصه.

He besieged his visitor with demands for future reports of dreams.
أنقل كاهل رائره بطلبات للحصول على نقارير مسمقبليه عن أحلامه.

This strange request bore regular and interesting fruit.

أثمر هذا الطلب الغريب نانج منظمة ومثيره للاهتمام.

***

After the first interview the manuscript records daily calls.
بعد المقابله الاولى، يسجل المخطوط المكالمات اليوميه.

He related startling fragments of nocturnal imagery.
روى مقاطع مدهله من صور ليليه.

There were always the same themes in his dreams.
كانت هناك دائماً نفس المواضيع فى أحلامه.

A terrible Cyclopean vista of dark and dripping stone.
مسهد مهيب صخم من الحجاره المظلمه المساقطه.

A subterranean voice or intelligence shouting monotonously.
صوت أو دكاء حمق يصرح برنابه.

Two sounds seemed to repeat themselves in his dreams.
بدا صوتان وكأنهما يتكرران فى أحلامه.

But these sounds were as enigmatic as the other sounds.
لكن هذه الاصوات كانت عامصه مثل الاصوات الاحرى.

The sounds can only be rendered by the letters "Cthulhu" and "R'lyeh".
لا يمكن نطق الأصوات إلا بواسطه الحرفين" كولو " و " ر'ليا"

On March 23rd, the manuscript continued, Wilcox failed to come.
فى 23 مارس، تابعت المحطوطه، لم يأب ويلكوكس.

My uncle made inquiries at the quarters of his whereabouts.
فام عمى بالاستفسار فى مقر إقامته عن مكان وجوده.

That night he had been stricken with an obscure sort of fever.
فى تلك الليله أصيب بنوع عامص من الحمى.

And he was taken to the home of his family in Waterman Street.
وتم نقله إلى مرل عائلته فى سارع ووترمان.

That night he had cried out in one of his dreams.

فن نلك الليله صرح فن أحد أحلامه.

His cries aroused several other artists in the building.

أنارت صرحانه حميطه العديد من الفاىيس الاحرين فن المبىى.

And he was between alternations of unconsciousness and delirium.

وكان بين نوباب من فمدان الوعن والهديان.

My uncle at once telephoned the family of Wilcox.

ابصل عمن على الفور بعابله ويلكوكس.

And from that time forward he kept close watch of the case.

ومد دلك الحين، طل يراقب المصيه عن كبس.

He called often at the Thayer Street office of Dr. Tobey.

كان يبردد كبيراً على مكبب الدكبور بوبن فن سارع باير.

Dr. Tobey was in charge of the patient's condition.

كان الدكبور بوبن مسوولا عن حاله المريص.

The youth's febrile mind was dwelling on strange things.

كان عمل الساب المصطرب يمكر فن أسباء عريبه.

The doctor shuddered now and then as he spoke of the dreams.

كان الطبيب يربجف بين الحين والآخر وهو يبحدب عن الأحلام.

The dreams repeated a lot of the earlier themes.

كررب الأحلام الكبير من المواصيع السابمه.

But now his dreams made mention of something new.

لكن أحلامه الان أسارب إلى سىء جديد.

A gigantic thing "a miles high" which walked, or lumbered about.

سىء عملاق "يبلغ اربماعه أميالاً" كان يمسن أو يبجول ببطء.

He at no time fully described this object in any detail.

لم يصف هدا السىء بسكل كامل أو ممصل فن أى وقب من الاوقاب.

But Dr. Tobey relayed the frantic words of his patient.

لكن الدكبور بوبن بمل الكلماب المدعوره لمريصه.

And the professor became increasingly certain of what it was.

وأصبح الأسئلة أكثر يقيناً مما كان عليه الأمر.

The nameless monstrosity he had sought to depict in his sculpture.

الوحس المجهول الذى سعى إلى تصويره فى منحوته.

The doctor had mentioned the bas-relief he had made.

وقد ذكر الطبيب النقس البارز الذى صنعه.

This mention preludes the young man's subsidence into lethargy.

يسير هذا الذكر إلى دحول الساب فى حاله من الحمول.

His temperature, oddly enough, was not greatly above normal.

والعريب فى الأمر أن درجة حرارته لم تكن أعلى بكبير من المعدل الطبيعى.

But his general condition suggested he was in a fever.

لكن حالته العامه أسارت إلى أنه كان يعانى من الحمى.

A fever, as opposed to being in the grasp of a mental disorder.

الحمى، على عكس الإصابه باصطراب عقلى.

***

On April 2nd at about 3 p.m. the fever came to an end.

فى الثانى من أبريل/نيسان، حوالى الساعه الثالثه مساء، انتهت الحمى.

Every trace of Wilcox's malady suddenly ceased.

احتفت كل آثار مرض ويلكوكس فجأه.

He sat upright in bed as if waking up from regular sleep.

جلس منتصباً فى السرير كما لو كان يستيقط من نوم عادى.

He was astonished to find himself at his parents' home.

لقد فوجى بوجوده فى مترل والديه.

And he was completely ignorant of what had happened.

وكان جاهلا تماماً بما حدث.

Neither dream nor reality had made an impression on his mind.

لم يترك الحلم ولا الواقع أى أثر فى ذهنه.

Dr. Tobey pronounced him fit to be dismissed from his care.
أعلن الدكتور توبئ أنه لابو للخروج من رعايته.

And he returned to his quarters three days later.
وعاد إلى مسكنه بعد ثلاثه أيام.

But to Professor Angell he was of no further assistance.
لكنه لم يقدم أى مساعده إضافيه للاساذ أنجيل.

All traces of strange dreaming had vanished with his recovery.
احتفت جميع آثار الأحلام الغريبه مع سفائه.

For a week he recounted irrelevant and thoroughly usual visions.
على مدار أسبوع، ظل يروى رؤى غير ذات صلة وعاديه تماماً.

And my uncle kept no further record of his night-thoughts.
ولم يحتفط عمى بأى سجل آخر لافكاره الليليه.

At this point the first part of the manuscript ended.
عند هذه النقطه انهى الجزء الاول من المخطوطه.

But my research was still anything but concluded.
لكن بحثى لم يكتمل بعد.

References to scattered notes helped piece things together.
ساعدت الإشارات إلى الملاحظات المسائره فى تجميع الامور معاً.

And there was more than enough material for thought.
وكان هناك ما يكفى من المواد للتفكير.

My distrust of the artist had still not subsided.
لم يزل عدم ثقتى بالفنان قائماً حتى الان.

But this was largely a result of my ingrained skepticism.
لكن هذا كان إلى حد كبير نتيجه لشكوكى المتأصله.

The notes described the dreams of various persons.
وصفت الملاحظات أحلام أسخاص محتلفين.

These dreams all occurred while young Wilcox was in his fever.
حدثت كل هذه الأحلام بينما كان الشاب ويلكوكس يعانى من الحمى.

My uncle, it seems, wasted no time in collecting the data.
يبدو أن عمى لم يضيع أى وقت فى جمع البيانات.

He had quickly instituted a prodigiously far-flung body of
inquiries.

لقد أنسأ بسرعه هيئه تحقيقات واسعه النطاق بسكل هائل.

Any friend that didn't show impertinence he questioned.

أى صديق لم يظهر وقاحه، كان يسجوبه.

He requested from them nightly reports of their dreams.

طلب منهم تقارير ليليه عن أحلامهم.

And he asked if they had had any notable visions of late.

وسألهم عما إذا كانت لديهم أى روى جديره بالذكر فى الاونه الاحيره.

The reception of his request seems to have been varied.

يبدو أن ردود الفعل على طلبه كانت متبايته.

But there was certainly no shortage in replies.

لكن بالـأكيد لم يكن هناك نقص فى الردود.

No ordinary man could have handled the replies alone.

لم يكن بإمكان أى رجل عادى التعامل مع الردود بمفرده.

The original correspondences were not preserved.

لم يتم الاحتفاظ بالمراسلات الاصليه.

But his notes formed a thorough and significant digest.

لكن ملاحظاته سكلت ملحصا ساملا وهاماً.

***

Initially he had approached average people in society.

فى البدايه، كان يتواصل مع عامه الناس فى المجتمع.

New England's traditional "salt of the earth".

"ملح الأرض" التقليدى فى نيو إنجلاند.

But this group gave an almost completely negative result.

لكن هذه المجموعه أعطت نتيجه سلبيه بسكل سبه كامل.

Though there were some exceptions to this group too.

مع ذلك، كانت هناك بعض الاستثناءات لهذه المجموعه أيضاً.

Scattered cases of uneasy but formless nocturnal
impressions.

حالات منفرقه من انطباعات ليليه مضطربه ولكنها غير محدده السكل.

Their reports were always between March 23rd and April 2nd.

كانت تقاريرهم دائماً ما تصدر بين 23 مارس و2 أبريل.

This aligned with the same period of young Wilcox's delirium.

تزامن هذا مع نفس فتره هذيان الساب ويلكوكس.

Men of science had been only a little more affected.

لم يتأثر رجال العلم إلا قليلا.

Though four cases of vague description were of interest.

على الرغم من أن أربع حالات ذات وصف غامض كانت مثيره للاهتمام.

They had had fugitive glimpses of strange landscapes.

لقد رأوا لمحات خاطفه من مناظر طبيعيه غريبه.

And in one case a dread of something abnormal was mentioned.

وفن إحدى الحالات، تم ذكر الخوف من سيء غير طبيعى.

It was from the artists and poets that the pertinent answers came.

جاءت الإجابات المناسبه من الفنانين والشعراء.

It is a blessing no one had been able to compare notes.

من حسن الحظ أنه لم يتمكن أحد من مقارنه المعلومات.

Panic would have broken loose had they shared their visions.

كان الذعر سينفجر لو أنهم شاركوا رؤاهم.

This, however, did not dispel my ingrained skepticism.

لكن هذا لم يبدد شكوكي المتأصله.

Others might have come to mythical conclusions much quicker.

ربما توصل آخرون إلى استنتاجات أسطوريه بسكل أسرع بكثير.

But the original letters were lacking from the notes.

لكن الرسائل الأصليه كانت مفقوده من الملاحظات.

I half suspected the compiler of having asked leading questions.

كتب أسك إلى حدّ ما فى أن جامع البياناب قد طرح أسله موجهه.

Or perhaps the correspondences weren't entirely original.
أو ربما لم نكن المراسلاب أصليه نماماً.

Perhaps my uncle had resolved to confirm Wilcox's dreams.
ربما كان عمن قد عزم على بأكيد أحلام ويلكوكس.

That is why I continued to feel suspicious of the sculptor.
ولهذا السبب اسمر سعورى بالريبه نجاه النحاب.

Perhaps he was still cognizant of my uncle's old data.
ربما كان لا يزال على درايه ببياناب عمن القديمه.

Perhaps he had been imposing on the veteran scientist.
ربما كان يفرض رأيه على العالم المحضرم.

Nonetheless, the corroborating data had to be investigated.
ومع دلك، كان لا بد من النحمق من البياناب المويده.

***

The responses from the esthetes told a disturbing tale.
كسمب ردود فعل أصحاب الدوو الرفيع عن قصه مقلمه.

From February 28th to April 2nd their dreams aligned.
من 28 فبراير إلى 2 أبريل، نلافب أحلامهم.

And a large proportion of them had dreamed very bizarre
things.
وقد حلمب نسبه كبيره منهم بأسياء عريبه للعايه.

The timing of the intensity of their dreams was also of
interest.
كان نوقيب سده أحلامهم ميراً للاهمام أيضاً.

The period of the sculptor's delirium marked a highpoint.
مثب فره هديان النحاب دروه فن مسيربه القيه.

The intensity of their dreams were immeasurably the
stronger.
كانب سده أحلامهم أقوى بكبير.

Over a quarter reported unfamiliar and unpronounceable
sounds.

أبلغ أكـر من ربع المساركين عن سماع أصواب عير مألوفه وعير قابله للطو.

Noises not dissimilar to what Wilcox had also described.
أصواب لا بحـلف كـيراً عما وصمه ويلكوكس أيصاً.

Some described highly elaborate and impossible architecture.
وصف البعص هدسه معماريه بالغه البعيد ومسحيله.

And some of the dreamers confessed to an acute fear.
واعـرف بعص الحالمين بسعورهم بحوف سديد.

Like Wilcox, they had seen some gigantic nameless thing.
ومسل ويلكوكس، فمد رأوا سيبا صحما بلا اسم.

One case, which the note describes with emphasis, was very sad.
إحدى الحالاب، البي بصمها المذكره بـأكيد، كانب محربه للعايه.

The subject was a widely known architect of the region.
كان السحص المعبن مهدساً معمارياً معروفاً على بطاو واسع فن المطمه.

He too had leanings toward theosophy and occultism.
كان لديه هو الاحر ميول بحو البيوصوفيا والسحر.

This man went violently insane on March the 22nd.
أصيب هدا الرجل بـوبه جبون عبيمه فن البانـي والعسريـن من مارس.

The exact same date of young Wilcox's seizure.
بمس باريح بوبه ويلكوكس الساب بالصبط.

He expired several months later, after incessant screaming..
بوفن بعد عده أسهر، إبر صراح مـواصل.

He begged to be saved from some escaped denizen of hell.
بوسل أن يبعد من أحد سكان الجحيم الهاربين.

Regrettably, my uncle did not refer to these cases by name.
للاسف، لم يذكر عمن هده المصايا بالاسم.

Instead, all studies were given nothing more than a number.
بدلا من دلك، لم بعط أى من الدراساب سوى رقم.

This way I was limited in attempting any personal investigation.
وبهده الطريمه، كـب محدوداً فن محاوله إجراء أى بحميو سححن.

And corroborating the evidence further was demanding.

وكان تأكيد الأدلة بسكل أكبر أمراً صعباً.

But finally I did succeed in tracing down some cases.
لكن نجحت في النهايه في تبع بعض الحالات.

I should have trusted the notes from my uncle.
كان ينبغي علي أن أثق بالملاحظات التي أرسلها عمي.

They reported their dreams true to their reports.
لقد نقلوا أحلامهم كما وردت في تقاريرهم.

I have often wondered what they thought the questioning meant.
لطالما تساءلت عما كانوا يعتقدون أن الاستجواب يعنيه.

It is for the best that no explanation shall ever reach them.
من الافضل ألا يصلهم أي تفسير على الإطلاق.

***

As I have mentioned, my uncle also collected press clippings.
كما ذكرت سابقاً، كان عمي أيضاً يجمع قصاصات الصحف.

These press clippings corresponded to the dates in question.
تتوافق هذه القصاصات الصحفيه مع التواريح المذكوره.

The sources were scattered throughout the globe.
كانت المصادر متفرقه في جميع أنحاء العالم.

Professor Angell must have employed a cutting bureau.
لا بد أن البروفيسور أنجيل قد استعان بمكتب تقطيع.

Because the number of extracts was tremendous.
لأن عدد المقتطفات كان هائلا.

There was a parallel to this part of his research.
كان هناك تشابه مع هذا الجزء من بحثه.

Cases of panic, mania, and eccentricity.
حالات الذعر والهوس والغرابه.

One case was a nocturnal suicide in London.
إحدى الحالات كانت انتحاراً ليلياً في لندن.

A lone sleeper had leaped from a window after a shocking cry.

قفز سحص نائم بمفرده من النافده بعد سماعه صرحه مروعه.

A rambling letter to the editor of a paper in South America.

رساله مطوله إلى رئيس تحرير إحدى الصحف فن أمريكا الجنوبيه.

A fanatic deduces a dire future from visions he had had.

يسسج متعصب مستقبلا قاتما من رؤى رآها.

A dispatch from California describes a theosophist colony.

تقرير من كاليفورنيا يصف مستعمره ثيوصوفيه.

They donned white robes en masse for some "glorious fulfilment".

ارتدوا أثواباً بيضاء جماعيه من أجل تحقيق "إنجار مجيد."

Although that "glorious fulfilment" never arose.

على الرعم من أن دلك "الإنجار المجيد" لم يتحقق قط.

There seems to be serious unrest from the natives in India.

يبدو أن هناك اضطرابات خطيره من جانب السكان الاصليين فن الهند.

Voodoo orgies multiplied in Haiti.

ترايدت حفلات الفودو الجسيه فن هايتن.

African outposts report ominous mutterings.

أفادت مواقع عسكريه أفريقيه بوجود همهمات تدر بالسوء.

American officers in the Philippines find certain tribes bothersome.

يجد الصباط الأمريكيون فن الفلبين أن بعض القبائل مزعجه.

New York policemen are mobbed by hysterical Levantines.

تعرض رجال سرطه نيويورك لمصايقات من قبل حسود من سكان بلاد الشام الهستيريين.

This occurred exactly on the night of March 22-23.

حدت هدا بالضبط فن ليله 22-23 مارس.

The west of Ireland, too, was full of wild rumor and legendry.

كان عرب أيرلندا أيضاً مليئاً بالشائعات والأساطير الجامحه.

A fantastic painter named Ardois-Bonnot made the news in France.

نصدر اسم رسام رابع يدعى أردوا بونو عاويس الأحبار فن فرسا.

He hung a blasphemous dream landscape in the Paris spring salon.

قام بتعليق لوحة حيالية ذات طابع تجديفن فن صالون الربيع فن باريس.

The recorded troubles in insane asylums were immeasurable.

كانت المساكل المسجله فن المصحات العقليه لا نُحصى.

A miracle must have kept the medical fraternities unsuspecting.

لا بد أن معجزه ما أبقت الأوساط الطبيه غافله.

But they never noted the strange parallelisms of the cases.

لكنهم لم يلاحظوا أبداً أوجه السابه العريبه بين الحالات.

Else they too would have come to mystified conclusions.

وإلا لكانوا هم أيضاً قد توصلوا إلى استساجات محيره.

I must confess these were indeed a set of weird paper cuttings.

لا بد لت من الاعتراف بأن هذه كانت بالفعل مجموعه من قصاصات الورق الغريبه.

My uncle had put forward a convincing argument.

لقد طرح عمن حجه مقنعه.

I can't explain how I set the evidence aside.

لا أسطيع أن أسرح كيف تجاهلت الادله.

But my callous rationalism took the upper hand.

لكن عقلانيتن الغاسيه سيطرت على الموقف.

And I was still suspicious of the young sculptor, Wilcox.

وما زلت أسك فن النحات الساب، ويلكوكس.

He must have known of the older matters mentioned by the professor.

لا بد أنه كان على علم بالأمور القديمه التن ذكرها الأستاد.

Let me turn your attention away from the young sculptor.
دعوني أحول انباهكم بعيدا عن النحات الساب.

And let us focus on the second half of the manuscript.
ولنركز الآن على النصف الثاني من المحطوطه.

A few dreams alone would not have been so significant.
لم نكن بعض الاحلام وحدها لنكون داب أهميه كبيره.

The bas-relief could have been dismissed as a hoax.
كان من الممكن اعبار النفس البارر مجرد حدعه.

But my uncle had previously been primed to take interest.
لكن عمني كان قد نم نهيسه مسبقاً لإبداء الاهنمام.

Wilcox's dream seemed to have a link to past events.
بدا أن حلم ويلكوكس مربط بأحداب الماصني.

It wasn't the first time that he had heard that word.
لم نكن هده المره الاولى النبي يسمع فيها نلك الكلمه.

The ominous syllables perhaps written as "Cthulhu".
ربما كُبب المقاطع المسوومه على سكل "كـمولو."

He had seen and heard of similar descriptions before.
لمد رأى وسمع أوصافاً مماثله من قبل.

The hellish outlines of the nameless monstrosity.
الحطوط الجهنميه للوحس المجهول.

He had previously puzzled over the same hieroglyphics.
لمد سبق له أن حيرنه نفس الهيروعليميه.

All this produced a horrible connection of events.
كل هدا أدى إلى سلسله مروعه من الاحداب.

It is no wonder he pursued young Wilcox with queries.
لا عجب أنه لاحق الساب ويلكوكس بالاسله.

And we must not be surprised he interrogated Wilcox so.
ولا يسبعن أن سماجاً بأنه اسـجوب ويلكوكس بهده الطريمه.

This earlier experience had come in the year of 1908.

وقد حدث هذه التجربه السابعه فى عام 1908.

Seventeen years before Wilcox came to my great-uncle.
قبل سبعه عشر عاما من مجئء ويلكوكس إلى عمى الاكبر.

The archeological society were meeting in St. Louis.
كانت الجمعيه الاثريه تجتمع فى سانت لويس.

Professor Angell had a prominent part in the deliberations.
كان للاستاد أنجيل دور بارز فى المداولات.

His responsibilities befitted one of his authority.
كانت مسوولياته تناسب مع مكانته وسلطته.

He was one of the first to be approached by several outsiders.
كان من أوائل من تواصل معهم العديد من الغرباء.

They took advantage of the convocation to offer questions.
استغلوا الاجتماع لطرح الاسئله.

They hoped for correct answering from an expert.
كانوا يأملون فى الحصول على إجابه صحيحه من خبير.

They each had very peculiar types of problems.
كان لكل منهم أنواع غريبه جداً من المساكل.

And they required very different types of solutions.
وقد تطلبت هذه الحلول أنواعاً مختلفه تماما.

The chief of these was a common-looking middle-aged man.
كان رئيس هولاء رجلا عادى المظهر فى منتصف العمر.

And he quickly became the meeting's focus of interest.
وسرعان ما أصبح محور اهتمام الاجتماع.

***

He had traveled to St. Louis all the way from New Orleans.
لقد سافر إلى سانت لويس من نيو أورليانز.

He had come to the meeting for special information.
لقد حضر الاجتماع للحصول على معلومات خاصه.

Knowledge that could not be unobtained from local source.

معرفه لا يمكن الحصول عليها من مصادر محليه.

His name was John Raymond Legrasse, police inspector.

كان اسمه جون ريموند ليغراس، مفتش شرطه.

He bore with him the mysterious subject of his inquiries.

كان يحمل معه موضوع استفساراته الغامض.

A grotesque and apparently very ancient stone statuette.

تمثال حجري غريب الشكل ويبدو أنه قديم جداً.

A statuette whose origin no one had been able to determine.

تمثال صغير لم يمكن أحد من تحديد أصله.

But don't assume Inspector Legrasse was an archeologist.

لكن لا تفترض أن المفتش ليغراس كان عالم آثار.

He had very little interest in archeology, nor mythology.

لم يكن لديه اهتمام كبير بعلم الآثار ولا بالاساطير.

His wish for enlightenment had rather different motivations.

كانت رغبته في التنوير مدفوعه بدوافع مختلفه تماماً.

He was prompted to come by purely professional considerations.

لقد دفعه إلى الحضور اعتبارات مهنيه بحته.

The statuette had been captured as part of a police raid.

تم الاستيلاء على التمثال كجزء من مداهمه للشرطه.

Although whether it was even a statuette wasn't determined.

على الرغم من أنه لم يتم تحديد ما إذا كان تمثالا صغيراً أم لا.

It could also have been an idol, magic fetish, or charm.

ربما كان أيضاً صنماً أو تميمه سحريه أو تعويذه.

Whatever it was, it had been captured some months previously.

أياً كان الأمر، فقد تم القبض عليه قبل بضعه أشهر.

A meeting was being held in the wooded swamps of New Orleans.

عُقد اجتماع في مستنقعات نيو أورليانز المشجره.

The police had been tipped of about a supposed voodoo meeting.

- 29 -

بلغت الشرطه بلاغاً عن اجتماع مزعوم للسعوده.

Strange and hideous rites connected with the voodoo circle.
طقوس غريبه وبشعه مرتبطه بدائره الفودو.

The police could not but realize what they had stumbled on.
لم يسع الشرطه إلا أن تدرك ما عثرت عليه بالصدفه.

A dark cult previously totally unknown to the authorities.
طائفه مظلمه كانت مجهوله تماماً للسلطات سابقاً.

Infinitely more sinister than what an outsider could expect.
أكثر شراً بكثير مما قد يتوقعه شخص غريب.

More diabolic than the blackest of the African voodoo circles.
أكثر شيطانيه من أحلك دوائر الفودو الأفريقيه.

Unbelievable tales were extorted from the captured cult members.
تم انتزاع قصص لا تصدق من أعضاء الطائفه الذين تم القبض عليهم.

But nothing of the relic's origin could be discovered.
لكن لم يتم اكتشاف أي شيء عن أصل الاثر.

Hence the anxiety of the police for any antiquarian lore.
ومن هنا يأتي قلق الشرطه بشأن أي معلومات أثريه.

Ancient mythology might explain the frightful symbol.
قد تفسر الاساطير القديمه هذا الرمز المخيف.

Deeper knowledge could perhaps track the fountain-head.
ربما يمكن للمعرفه الأعمق أن تتعقب منبعها.

Inspector Legrasse was not prepared for the excitement he created.
المفتش ليجراس مستعداً للإثاره التي أحدثها.

One sight of the mysterious object was all that was required.
كانت رؤيه واحده للشيء الغامض كافيه.

The assembled men of science were filled with curiosity.
امتلأ رجال العلم المجتمعون بالفضول.

They lost no time in crowding closely around the inspector.
لم يضيعوا أي وقت في التجمع حول المفتش.

And they all tried to get the best look at the diminutive figure.

وحاولوا جميعاً الحصول على أفضل نظره على دلك السكل الصغير.

***

The genuinely abysmal antiquity inspired wild imagination.

لقد ألهمت تلك الحقبه القديمه الباسه حقاً حيالا جامحاً.

The strangeness hinted so potently at unopened and archaic vistas.

لقد أوحت الغرابه بقوه إلى آفاق لم تُفتح بعد وأخرى عتيقه.

No recognized school of sculpture had animated this terrible object.

لم تقم أى مدرسه نحت معرف بها بإضفاء الحيويه على هذا الشىء الرهيب.

Yet centuries seemed recorded in the dim and greenish surface.

لكن يبدو أن قروناً قد سجلت على السطح الباهت ذى اللون الأخضر.

Perhaps thousands of years were hidden in this unplaceable stone.

ربما كانت آلاف السنين محفيه فى هذا الحجر الذى لا يمكن وضعه.

The figurine was finally passed slowly from man to man.

وأخيراً، تم تمرير التمثال ببطء من رجل إلى آخر.

Each scientist carefully studied the strange markings of the stone.

قام كل عالم بدراسه العلامات الغريبه الموجوده على الحجر بعنايه.

The work was between seven and eight inches in height.

كان ارتفاع العمل الفنى يتراوح بين سبعه وثمانيه بوصات.

And the exquisite artistic workmanship must be noted.

ويجب الإشاره إلى الحرفيه الفنيه الرائعه.

The carvings represented a monster of vaguely anthropoid outline.

كانت المنحوتات تمثل وحشاً ذا شكل بشرى غامض.

On the face of the octopus-esque head was a mass of feelers.

على وجه الرأس السبيه بالأحطبوط كله من المجساب.

Prodigious claws on hind and fore feet protruded from the body.

كانب محالب ضحمه نبرر من الجسم، سواء فن القدمين الحلفيه أو الأماميه.

The bloated corpulence had a rubbery looking quality to it.

كان للجسد المسمح مطهر مطاطن.

And from behind the rubbery body came out two narrow wings.

ومن حلف الجسم المطاطن حرج جماحان صيفان.

It would be instinctual to think of this thing as fearsome.

سيكون من الطبيعن أن نعبر هذا السىء محيفاً.

There was an unnatural malignancy to the aura of the creature.

كان هاك نوع من الحبب عير الطبيعن فن هاله المحلوق.

The gargantuan squatted evilly on a rectangular block.

جلس العملاو بسكل سرير على كله مسطيله.

The pedestal it was on was covered with undecipherable characters.

كانب القاعده التن كان عليها معطاه برمور عير قابله للمراءه.

The tips of the wings touched the back edge of the block.

لامسب أطراف الاجنحه الحافه الحلفيه للكله.

The creature was sitting on the middle of the giant block.

كان المحلوق يجلس فن مصف الكله العملافه.

Its legs were doubled up under its monstrous body.

كانب ساقاه مطويين نحب جسده الوحسن.

The long, curved claws gripped the front edge of the cliff.

سبب المحالب الطويله المحنيه بالحافه الاماميه للجرف.

The cephalopod head was bent forward, observing its kingdom.

كان رأس رأسياب الأرجل محنيا إلى الأمام، يراقب مملكه.

The ends of the facial feelers brushed the backs of huge forepaws.

لامس أطراف قرون الاسسعار الوجهيه الجرء الحلفن من الكفوف الأماميه الصحمه.

And the forepaws clasped the croucher's elevated knees.
وأمسك المحالب الاماميه بركبتى الكلب المحنى المرفوعين.

The appearance of the grotesque scene was abnormally lifelike.
كان مظهر المسهد العريب واقعياً بسكل عير طبيعى.

But this lifelike quality only added a subtle reason to be more fearful.
لكن هده الصفه الواقعيه لم نصف سوى سبب حفى لمريد من الحوف.

Because we knew nothing about the source of the depiction,
لانا لم نكن نعرف سيئاً عن مصدر الصوره.

The creature's vast, awesome, and incalculable age was unmistakable.
كان عمر المحلوق الهائل والمهيب والدى لا يمكن حسابه واصحاً لا لبس فيه.

But not one link did the depiction show with any known type of art.
لكن لم يطهر أى رابط بين هدا التصوير وأى نوع معروف من الفنون.

Not even the earliest civilizations made reference to this creature.
لم ندكر حنى أفدم الحضاراب هدا المحلوق.

But that is not the only point at which our knowledge failed us.
لكن هده ليسب النقطه الوحيده التى حدلنا فيها معرفنا.

***

The mineralogy of the stone was also a complete mystery.
كانب المعادن المكونه للحجر لعراً كاملا أيضاً.

Gold specks dotted the soapy, greenish-black stone.
كانب بقع الدهب نبائر على الحجر دى اللون الاحضر الداكن المائل إلى السواد.

Iridescent striations ran along the length of the stone.
امدب حطوط مفرحه الالوان على طول الحجر.

In short, the stone resembled nothing within mineralogy.

باختصار، لم يكن الحجر يشبه أي شيء في علم المعادن.

Geologists hadn't been able to identify the stone either.

لم يتمكن الجيولوجيون من تحديد نوع الحجر أيضاً.

The hieroglyphs along the stone were equally baffling.

كانت النقوش الهيروغليفيه على طول الحجر محيره بنفس القدر.

The writing system was horribly different than other scripts.

كان نظام الكتابه مختلفا تماما عن أنظمه الكتابه الاخرى.

A representation of half the world's leading experts was present.

حضر ممثلون عن نصف كبار الخبراء في العالم.

But no link to any known writing system could be established.

لكن لم يتم التوصل إلى أي صله بأي نظام كتابه معروف.

Everything frightfully suggested an old and unhallowed cycle of life.

كل شيء يوحي بشكل مرعب بدوره حياه قديمه وغير مقدسه.

A history in which our world and our conceptions played no part.

تاريخ لم يلعب فيه عالمنا ومفاهيمنا أي دور.

The experts shook their heads, admitting they had been defeated.

هز الخبراء رووسهم، معترفين بهزيمتهم.

But one expert did not give up quite so quickly.

لكن أحد الخبراء لم يستسلم بهذه السرعه.

He claimed to have a touch of bizarre familiarity with the subject.

وادعى أنه يملك معرفه غريبه بالموضوع.

The monstrous shape and writing weren't entirely new to him.

لم يكن الشكل الوحشي والكتابه غريبين عليه تماماً.

With some diffidence he told of the odd trifle he knew.

وبشيء من التردد، روى بعض الامور التافهه الغريبه التي كان يعرفها.

This person was the late William Channing Webb.

كان هذا السحص هو الراحل ويليام سانيع ويب.

He was professor of anthropology in Princeton University.

كان أسادا لعلم الإسان فن جامعه بريسسون.

And he was an explorer of no small significance.

وكان مسكسفا دا أهميه بالعه.

***

Forty-eight years ago he was exploring Greenland and
Iceland.

قبل نمانيه وأربعين عاما كان يسكسف عريلاند وأيسلدا.

His group were in search of some Runic inscriptions.

كانت مجموعته نبحت عن بعص النقوس الرونيه.

But the expedition failed to unearth any inscriptions.

لكن البعنه فسلت فن العنور على أى نقوس.

They trekked the heights of West Greenland's coasts.

لقد جابوا مرنفعات سواحل عرب جريلاند.

Here they encountered a strange cult of degenerate Eskimos.

وهنا صادفوا طانفه عريبه من الإسكيمو المنحطين.

Their religion consisted of a form of devil-worship.

كان دينهم يأالف من سكل من أسكال عباده السيطان.

And their rituals were deliberately bloodthirsty and
repulsive.

وكانت طقوسهم دمويه ومقرره عن قصد.

It was a faith of which other Eskimos knew little.

كان دلك دينا لم يكن الإسكيمو الاحرون يعرفون عنه الكير.

Locals shuddered at the mention of their practices.

ارنجف السكان المحليون عند دكر ممارسانهم.

They said their believes came from horribly ancient eons.

قالوا إن معسقدانهم نعود إلى عصور قديمه مرعبه.

A time before the world as we know it now had ever been
made.

رمز قبل أن يَحلو العالم كما نعرفه الآن.

There were human sacrifices and queer hereditary rituals.

كانت هناك تضحيات بشريه وطقوس ورايه غريبه.

And all their worship was directed at a supreme tornasuk.

وكانت كل عبادتهم موجهه إلى إله عظيم.

Professor Webb had taken a phonetic copy from an aged angekok.

أحد البروفيسور ويب نسخة صوتيه من أنجيكوك قديم.

He had transcribed the wizard-priest's chants as best he could.

لقد قام بنسخ ترانيم الكاهن الساحر بأفضل ما استطاع.

But currently these transcriptions weren't of prime significance.

لكن هذه النسخ لم تكن ذات أهميه كبيره في الوقت الحالي.

The cult had a cherished stone that they worshipped.

كان لدى الطائفه حجر عزيز كانوا يعبدونه.

They danced wildly when the aurora leaped over the ice cliffs.

رقصوا بجنون عندما قفز الشفق القطبي فوق المنحدرات الجليديه.

And in the midst of their dance was the strange stone.

وفي خضم رقصهم كان الحجر الغريب.

It was, the professor stated, a very crude bas-relief of stone.

وذكر الاستاد أنها كانت نحته حجريه بدائيه للغايه.

The stone comprised a hideous picture and some cryptic writing.

كان الحجر يحمل صوره بشعه وبعض الكتابات الغامضه.

And as far as he could tell this stone was a rough parallel.

وبحسب ما استطاع أن يدركه، كان هذا الحجر بمثابه نظير تقريبي.

The stone had all the same essential features of bestial things.

كان الحجر يحمل جميع السمات الأساسيه نفسها للأشياء الوحشيه.

The scientists received this data with suspense and astonishment.

استقبل العلماء هذه البيانات بترقب ودهشه.

Even Inspector Legrasse had quickly gained an interest in mythology.

حتى المفتش ليغراس سرعان ما أبدى اهتماماً بالأساطير.

And he began at once to ply his informant with questions.

وبدأ على الفور في توجيه الاسئله إلى محبره.

He had notes of the oral ritual of the cult-worshipers in the swamp.

كان لديه ملاحظات عن الطقوس الشفويه لعباده الطوائف في المستنقع.

He besought the professor to remember the diabolist Eskimos' chants.

توسل إلى الأستاذ أن يتذكر ترانيم الإسكيمو الشيطانيه.

There then followed an exhaustive comparison of details.

ثم تلا ذلك مقارنه شامله للتفاصيل.

And there then followed a moment of really awed silence.

ثم تلا ذلك لحظه من الصمت المهيب.

The Eskimo wizards and the Louisiana swamp-priests were worlds apart.

كان سحره الإسكيمو وكهنه مستنقعات لويزيانا عالمين منفصلين تماماً.

And yet there was a phrase the two hellish rituals had in common.

ومع ذلك، كانت هناك عباره مشتركه بين الطقوس الجهنميه.

"Ph'nglui mglw'nafh Cthulhu R'lyeh wgah'nagl fhtagn."

"فعلوئي" معلو نف كتالهو ر'ليه ووعاه ناعل فهتاجن.

***

Legrasse had one advantage over Professor Webb.

ليغراس ميزه واحده على البروفيسور ويب.

He had spoken to several of his mongrel prisoners.

لقد تحدث إلى العديد من سجنائه من ذوي الاصول المختلطه.

Some of them had passed on the phrase's meaning.

وقد نقل بعضهم معنى العباره.

"In his house at R'lyeh dead Cthulhu waits dreaming."
"فى مىرله فى رليه، يسطر كاىولو الميب حالما".

So the attention turned back to Inspector Legrasse.
وهكدا عاد الاهمام إلى المفىس ليعراس.

And he was probed with many disconnected questions.
ونم اسجوابه بالعديد من الاسله المعرفه.

He detailed his experience with the worshipers from the
swamp.
وقد سرد بالىفصيل نجربه مع المصلين الفادمين من المسىقع.

My uncle attached profound significance to the story.
أولى عمى أهميه بالعه لهده الفصه.

The report savored of the wildest dreams of myth-makers.
كان الىقرير أسبه بأحلام صاع الاساطير الجامحه.

Theosophists could not have provided more imagination.
لم يكن بإمكان أنباع الىيوصوفيه أن يقدموا حيالا أكىر من دلك.

But the philosophies came from unexpected sources.
لكن هذه الفلسفاب جاءب من مصادر عير مىوقعه.

Half-castes and pariahs told these fantastical stories.
روى المبودون والمحدرون من أصول محلطه هذه الفصص الحياليه.

On November 1st, 1907, his chain of events unfolded.
فى الأول من ىوفمبر عام 1907، بدأب سلسله الاحداب ىكسف.

The New Orleans police received desperate calls.
ىلقب سرطه ىيو أورليانر مكالمات اسعابه.

They were called to the swamp and lagoon country to the
south.
ىم اسدعاوهم إلى مىطقه المسىقعاب والبحيراب فى الجىوب.

The settlers there were mostly primitive, but good-natured.
كان المسىوطنون هناك فى العالب بدابيين، لكىهم طيبو الفلب.

Most living by the swamp were descendants of Lafitte's
men.
كان معطم سكان المىطقه المحيطه بالمسىقع من ىسل رجال لافيب.

But now they were in the grip of stark terror.
لكىهم الآن واقعون نحب وطأه رعب سديد.

An unknown thing had stolen upon them in the night.

لقد تسلل إليهم سىء مجهول فى الليل.

It was voodoo, apparently, that caused the disturbance.

يبدو أن السحر الاسود هو الذى تسبب فى هذا الاصطراب.

But it was a voodoo unlike the other forms of voodoo.

لكنها كانت طقوساً سحريه تختلف عن الاسكال الاخرى للسحر الاسود.

Voodoo of a more terrible sort than they had ever known.

سحر الفودو من نوع أفطع مما عرفوه من قبل.

Some of their women and children had disappeared.

احتفى بعص نسائهم وأطفالهم.

A malevolent drumming had begun its incessant beating...

بدأ قرع طبول حبيب بدفائه المتواصله.

Far and deep within those dark, black haunted woods.

فى أعماق تلك الغابات المطلمه السوداء المسكونه.

There, where no dweller dared to ventured close to.

هناك، حيب لم يجرو أى ساكن على الاقتراب.

There were insane shouts and harrowing screams.

كانت هناك صيحات جنونيه وصراح مروع.

Soul-chilling chants and dancing devil-flames,

ترانيم تقسعر لها الابدان ولهيب سيطانى راقص.

The messenger and his people could stand it no more.

لم يعد بإمكان الرسول وقومه تحمل ذلك.

A body of twenty police set out in the late afternoon.

انطلقت مجموعه من عسرين سرطياً فى وقت متأخر من بعد الظهر.

And a shivering settler came with them as a guide.

وجاء معهم مستوطن يرتجف من البرد كدليل.

***

At the end of the passable road they alighted.

ترجلوا عند نهايه الطريق الصالح للمرور.

For miles and miles they splashed on in silence.

اسمروا فى اللويح بأميال وأميال فى صمت.

And they went on through the terrible cypress woods.
وواصلوا سيرهم عبر عابات السرو الرهيبه.

Dark, dark woods in which day but almost never came.
عابات مطلمه، مطلمه، لم يأب فيها النهار إلا نادراً.

Ugly roots set traps for them in the wet ground.
نصب الجدور القبيحه فخاخاً لهم فى الارض الرطبه.

Malignant hanging nooses of Spanish moss beset them.
أحاطت بهم حبال خبيثه من الطحالب الإسبانيه المتدليه.

In the distance the settlement slowly came into sight.
بدأت المستوطنه تظهر ببطء فى الافق البعيد.

Hysterical dwellers ran out of the miserable huts.
فرّ السكان الهستيريون من الاكواح الباسه.

They clustered around the group of bobbing lanterns.
وتجمعوا حول مجموعه الفوانيس المأرجحه.

Far, far ahead the cause of all the fear could be heard.
من بعيد، من بعيد، كان بالإمكان سماع سبب كل هذا الحوف.

The muffled beat of drums was now faintly audible.
أصبح صوت الطبول المكتوم مسموعاً بسكل حافت.

At times the wind shifted and revealed different sounds.
فى بعض الاحيان، كانت الرياح تتغير وتكسف عن أصوات محتلفه.

Curdling shrieks were audible at infrequent intervals.
كانت الصرخات المروعه مسموعه على فترات متباعده.

A reddish glare seemed to filter through the undergrowth.
بدا وكأن وهجاً محمراً يتسلل عبر السجيرات.

The settlers were reluctant to be left alone again.
كان المستوطنون مترددين فى أن يتركوا وحدهم مره أخرى.

But they point blank refused to move forwards either.
لكنهم رفضوا بسكل قاطع المضى قدماً أيضاً.

So the inspector and his colleagues plunged on unguided.
وهكذا انطلق المفتس ورملاوه دون توجيه.

And they went into the black arcades of horror.

ودخلوا إلى أروقّه الرعب المظلمه.

The region was one of traditionally evil repute.
كانت المنطقه ذات سمعه سيئه تقليدياً.

The lands were substantially unknown by white men.
كانت هذه الاراضي مجهوله إلى حد كبير بالنسبه للرجال البيض.

Not many explorers had traversed those regions yet.
لم يقم الكثير من المستكشفين باجتياز تلك المناطق بعد.

There were also legends of a hidden away lake.
كان هناك أيضاً أساطير عن بحيره مخفيه.

A body of water still unglimpsed by mortal sight.
مسطح مائي لا يزال بعيد عن أنظار البشر.

In the lake it was said there dwelt a strange creature.
قيل إن البحيره كان تسكنها مخلوقات غريبه.

A huge, formless white polypous thing with luminous eye.
شحم أبيض متعدد الاشكال عديم الشكل ذو عين مضيئه.

And settlers whispered about bat-winged devils.
وتناقل المستوطنون همساً عن شياطين بأجنحه الخفافيس.

They flew up out of caverns from the inner earth.
لقد طاروا من الكهوف من باطن الارض.

And together the demons worship it at midnight.
وتجتمع الشياطين لتعبدها في منتصف الليل.

They said it had been there before D'Iberville.
قالوا إنها كانت موجوده هناك قبل دي إيبرفيل.

They said it had been there before La Salle too.
قالوا إنها كانت موجوده قبل لاسال أيضاً.

They said it was there before the Native Americans.
قالوا إنها كانت موجوده قبل وصول السكان الاصليين لامريكا.

Perhaps it was even there before the wholesome beasts.
ربما كان موجوداً حتى قبل ظهور الوحوش الطيبه.

It was a nightmare itself that made men dream.
لقد كان كابوساً بحد ذاته هو الذي جعل الرجال يحلمون.

And to see the thing was the same as death.

ورويه ذلك السيء كانت بمثابة الموت.

And so they had enough warning to know to keep away.
وهكذا كان لديهم ما يكمن من التحذير ليعرفوا أن عليهم الابتعاد.

Because it was indeed where they were warned it was.
لأنه كان بالفعل المكان الذى تم تحذيرهم منه.

The voodoo orgy was on the fringe of this abhorred area.
كانت طقوس الفودو الجنسيه على هامش هذه المنطقه البغيضه.

But the location was already bad enough by itself.
لكن الموقع كان سيئاً بما فيه الكفايه فى حد ذاته.

The voodoo activities only added to the horror.
لم تزد طقوس الفودو إلا من الرعب.

Perhaps poetry could do justice to the noises heard.
لعل الشعر يستطيع أن يصف الاصوات المسموعه وصفاً وافياً.

Otherwise only madness would help one understand.
وإلا فإن الجنون وحده هو ما سيساعد المرء على الفهم.

But Legrasse's plowed on through the black morass.
لكن ليغراس واصل طريقه عبر المستنقع الاسود.

The sound of the muffled drumming slowly crystalized.
بدأ صوت قرع الطبول المكتوم يتبلور ببطء.

And they continued steadily towards the red glare.
واستمروا فى السير بثبات نحو الوهج الاحمر.

***

There are vocal qualities specific to men.
هناك خصائص صوتيه خاصه بالرجال.

And there are vocal qualities specific to beasts.
وهناك خصائص صوتيه خاصه بالحيوانات.

It is terrible when one makes the sounds of the other...
إنه لأمر فظيع عندما يقلد أحدهما أصوات الاخر.

Animal fury freed them of their human restraint.
أحررهم غضب الحيوانات من قيودهم البشريه.

Orgiastic license whipped them into demoniac heights.

أدى التحرر الجنسي المفرط إلى دفعهم إلى مستويات شيطانيه.

Howls that tore through those perpetually dark woods.

عواء مزق تلك الغابات المظلمه على الدوام.

Squawking ecstasies that echoed in everyone's mind.

صرخات نشوه ترددت أصداؤها في أذهان الجميع.

Sounds like pestilential tempests from the gulfs of hell,

يبدو الامر وكأنه عواصف وبائيه قادمه من أعماق الجحيم.

Now and then the less organized ululations would cease.

بين الحين والاخر، كانت الزعاريد الاقل تنظيماً تتوقف.

A well-drilled chorus of hoarse voices rose in singsong.

ارتفعت جوقه من الاصوات الحسه المدربه جيداً في غناء متناغم.

And they chanted that hideous phrase of their ritual.

ورددوا تلك العباره البشعه من طقوسهم.

"Ph'nglui mglw'nafh Cthulhu R'lyeh wgah'nagl fhtagn".

"فنجلوي" مغلو نف كثالهو رلّيه ووغاه ناغل فهتاجن.

Then the men reached a spot where the trees were sparser.

ثم وصل الرجال إلى مكان كانت فيه الاشجار أقل كثافه.

Suddenly they come in sight of the spectacle itself.

وفجأه أصبحوا على مرأى من المشهد نفسه.

Four of them reeled from the horrible things they saw.

أصيب أربعه منهم بالذهول من الاشياء المروعه التي رأوها.

One man fainted, and two were shaken into a frantic cry.

أغمي على رجل، وهز رجلان حتى صرخا صراخاً هستيرياً.

Fortunately their screams were not heard by other ears.

لحسن الحظ، لم تسمع آذان أخرى صرخاتهم.

The mad cacophony of the orgy deadened their screams.

أخمدت الضوضاء الصاخبه للحفله الجنسيه صرخاتهم.

Legrasse splashed swamp water on the fainting man.

ليغراس برش مياه المستنقع على الرجل الذي أغمي عليه.

They stood up again, but nearly hypnotized with horror.

نهضوا مره أخرى، لكنهم كانوا شبه مسحورين من شده الرعب.

In a natural glade of the swamp stood a grassy island.

في فسحه طبيعيه من المستنقع، كانت نصف جزيره عشبيه.

The grassy island extended perhaps for an acre.
امتد الجزيره العشبيه ربما لمسافه فدان.

And the area was clear of trees and tolerably dry.
وكانت المنطقه خاليه من الاشجار وجافه إلى حد معقول.

A horde of human abnormality leaped and twisted.
قفزت مجموعه من الكائنات البشريه الشاذه والتوت.

No Sime could paint what the men were seeing.
لا يمكن لأي فنان أن يرسم ما كان يراه الرجال.

No Angarola has ever painted such an indescribable scene.
لم يسبق لأي من فناني أنجارولا أن رسم مشهداً لا يوصف كهذا.

The hybrid spawn made a monstrous ring-shaped bonfire.
أشعلت المخلوقات الهجينه ناراً ضخمه على شكل حلقه.

They brayed bellowed and writhed about in their nudity.
كانوا يصيحون ويهدرون ويتلوون وهم عراه.

Occasionally there were rifts in the curtain of flame.
كانت تظهر بين الحين والاخر سموق في ساره اللهب.

And there the object of their worship revealed itself.
وهناك تجلى لهم معبودهم.

In the midst of the fire stood a great granite monolith.
وسط النيران، وقفت صخره ضخمه من الجرانيت.

The stone structure was only about eight feet in height.
لم يتجاوز ارتفاع الهيكل الحجري ثمانيه أقدام.

And the noxious carven statuette rested on the monolith.
واستقر التمثال المنحوت الضار على الصخره الضخمه.

The idle was almost incongruous in its diminutiveness.
كان التمثال شبه متنافر في ضآلته.

Spaced evenly, scaffolds had been erected around the fire.
تم نصب سقالات حول النار على مسافات متساويه.

From the scaffolding hung a number of marred bodies.
تدلى عدد من الجثث المشوهه من السقالات.

The bodies of those that had disappeared from nearby.

جب أولئك الذين احتفوا من المنطقه المجاوره.

It was inside this circle the ring of worshipers were.
كانت حلقه المصلين داخل هذه الدائره.

And they roared and jumped in the frantic trance.
وهدروا وقفزوا فى حاله من الهلع الشديد.

The general direction of the motion was anti-clockwise.
كان الاتجاه العام للحركه عكس اتجاه عقارب الساعه.

The ring of bodies circling around the ring of fire.
حلقه من الأجساد تدور حول حلقه النار.

One man recollected other details even more concerning.
وتذكر رجل آخر تفاصيل أخرى أكثر إثاره للقلق.

But perhaps the echoes induced him to hear other things.
لكن ربما دفعته الاصداء إلى سماع أشياء أخرى.

He fancied he heard antiphonal responses to the ritual.
تخيل أنه سمع ردوداً متبادله على الطقوس.

Noises from an unillumined spot deeper within the woods.
أصوات قادمه من بقعه مظلمه فى أعماق الغابه.

This man, Joseph D. Galvez, I later met and questioned.
هذا الرجل، جوزيف د. غالفير، قابلته لاحقاً واستجوبته.

And he proved to indeed be distractingly imaginative.
وقد أثبت بالفعل أنه يتمتع بخيال واسع يشتت الانتباه.

He even hinted at the faint beating of great wings.
بل إنه ألمح إلى خفقان خافت لأجنحه عظيمه.

And he suggested there was a glimpse of shining eyes.
وأشار إلى أنه رأى لمحه من عيون لامعه.

And beyond the trees, a mountainous white bulk of
something.
وخلف الأشجار، كتله بيضاء جبليه من شىء ما.

I suppose he had heard too much native superstition.
أظن أنه سمع الكثير من الخرافات المحليه.

But actually the horrified pause was relatively brief.
لكن فى الواقع، كان الصمت المرعب قصيراً نسبياً.

Duty came first, and they had come to do a job.

كان الواجب هو الأولويه، وقد جاووا للقيام بمهمه.

***

There must have been nearly a hundred mongrel celebrants.
لا بد أن عدد المحتفلين كان يقارب المئه من ذوى الاصول المختلطه.

But the police were able to rely on their firearms.
لكن السرطه تمكنت من الاعتماد على أسلحتها الناريه.

And they plunged determinedly into the nauseous rout.
وانخرطوا بعزم فى الهزيمه المقيته.

For five minutes the chaotic din was beyond description.
لمده خمس دقائق، كان الصجيج الفوضوى يفوق الوصف.

Wild blows were struck and shots were fired.
وُجّهت ضربات عنيفه وأطلقت أعيره ناريه.

Some escaped arrest by running into the darkness.
تمكن البعض من الفرار من الاعتقال باللجوء إلى الظلام.

They had a better knowledge of the layout of the swamp.
كان لديهم معرفه أفضل بتخطيط المستنقع.

But Legrasse and his men caught around half of them.
لكن ليغراس ورجاله تمكنوا من القبض على حوالى نصفهم.

And they counted around forty-seven sullen prisoners.
وأحصوا حوالى سبعه وأربعين سجينا كئيبا.

They were forced to put on their clothes again.
أجبروا على ارتداء ملابسهم مره أخرى.

And they fell into line between two rows of policemen.
واصطفوا بين صفين من رجال السرطه.

Five of the worshipers lay dead by the fire.
خمسه من المصلين لقوا حتفهم بجانب النار.

Two severely wounded prisoners were carried away.
تم نقل سجينين مصابين بجروح خطيره.

Of course the image on the monolith was removed.
وبالطبع تمت إزاله الصوره من على الصخره الضخمه.

Legrasse himself took the evidence to the police station.

ليغراس بنفسه بأحد الادله إلى مركز الشرطه.

The trip back to the headquarters was of intense strain.

كانت رحله العوده إلى المقر الرئيسي رحله شاقه للغايه.

The men were examined when they got back to civilization.

تم فحص الرجال عندما عادوا إلى الحضاره.

The prisoners all proved to be men of a very low type.

تبين أن جميع السجناء كانوا رجالا من نوع وضيع للغايه.

They were all mixed-blooded, and mentally aberrant.

كانوا جميعاً من دوي الاصول المختلطه، ويعانون من اضطرابات عقليه.

Most were seamen by trade, or some similar professions.

كان معظمهم بحاره بحكم مهنهم، أو من أصحاب مهن مماثله.

Negroes and mulattoes were sprinkled among them.

كان الزنوج والملونون منتشرين بينهم.

But most seemed to be West Indians or Brava Portuguese.

لكن يبدو أن معظمهم كانوا من سكان جزر الهند العربيه أو البرتغاليين من برافا.

They primarily came from the Cape Verde Islands.

كانوا في الأساس من جزر الرأس الاخضر.

They gave the heterogeneous cult a coloring of voodooism.

لقد أضفوا على هذه الطائفه المتنوعه طابعاً من السحر الاسود.

But there wasn't even a need to ask too many questions.

لكن لم تكن هناك حاجه حتى لطرح الكثير من الاسئله.

The conclusion quickly became manifest by itself.

سرعان ما اتضحت النتيجه من تلقاء نفسها.

Something far deeper than negro fetishism was involved.

كان الامر أعمق بكثير من مجرد تقديس الزنوج.

Although ignorant, but their story was consistent.

على الرغم من جهلهم، إلا أن قصصهم كانت متسقه.

The creatures all spoke of the same central idea.

تحدثت جميع المخلوقات عن نفس الفكره المركزيه.

They certainly all shared the same loathsome faith.

لقد كانوا جميعاً يشتركون في نفس المعتقد البغيض.

They worshiped, so they said, the great old ones.

كانوا يعبدون، كما قالوا، الكائنات القديمه العظيمه.

The great old ones lived long before there were any men.
لقد عاست الكائنات القديمه العظيمه قبل وجود أى رجال برمن طويل.

And they came to the young world out of the sky.
وجاووا إلى العالم الفتى من السماء.

Those old ones were now gone, they explained.
وأوضحوا أن تلك القديمه قد احتفت الان.

They were now inside the earth and under the sea.
لقد كانوا الآن داخل الارض وتحت سطح البحر.

But their dead bodies found ways to tell their secrets.
لكن جسهم وجدت طرقاً للكسف عن أسرارهم.

They whispered into the dreams of the first men.
همسوا فن أحلام الرجال الاوائل.

And the first men formed a cult which has never died.
وسكّل الرجال الاوائل طائفه لم تمت فط.

***

The cult had always existed, and always would exist.
لطالما وجدت هده الطائفه، وسطل موجوده دائما.

Their followers were hidden in wastes all over the world.
كان أتباعهم يحتبون فن الاراضن القاحله فن جميع أنحاء العالم.

Their followers were in dark places explorers overlooked.
كان أتباعهم فن أماكن مطلمه أغملها المستكسفون.

And they would remain hidden until they were called.
وسيطللون محتبيين حتى يتم استدعاوهم.

When the great priest Cthulhu rises again to the surface.
عندما يعود الكاهن العطيم كولو إلى السطح.

When Cthulhu brings the earth again beneath his sway.
عندما يحضع كاولو الارض مره أخرى لسلطانه.

When Cthulhu leaves from his dark house in the mighty city of R'lyeh.

عدما يعادر كابولو مرله المطلم فن مديبه رليه العطيمه.

Some day he was going call, when the stars were ready.
سيأبن يوم يبصل فيه، عدما نكون النجوم جاهره.

And the secret cult will always be waiting to liberate him.
وسطل الطابفه السريه سطر دابماً لـحريره.

Meanwhile, no more of his story must be told.
وفن الوقب نفسه، لا يجب سرد المريد من قصسه.

There was a secret even torture could not extract.
كان هناك سرّ حسى النعديب لم يسطع اسراعه.

Mankind was not alone among the conscious things of earth.
لم يكن البسر وحدهم بين الكاسات الواعيه على الارص.

Because shapes came out of the dark to visit the faithful few.
لان الاسكال حرجب من الطلام لرياره الفله المومسه.

But these were not the great old ones.
لكن هولاء لم يكونوا العطماء الفدامى.

No man had ever seen the great old ones.
لم يرَ أئ إسان الكاساب الفديمه العطيمه فط.

The carven idol was of great Cthulhu.
كان الصم المسحوب يمبل كابولو العطيم.

None could say whether the others were like him.
لم يسطع أحد أن يجرم ما إدا كان الاحرون مبله.

No one could read the old writing now.
لم يعد بإمكان أحد قراءه الكبابه الفديمه الان.

Instead, things were told by word of mouth.
بدلاً من دلك، كابب الامور نبل سفهياً.

The chanted ritual was not the secret.
لم يكن السر فن الطفوس البن بردد.

The secret was never spoken aloud, only whispered.
لم يبطق السر بصوت عال فط، بل بم همسه فقط.

The chant meant one thing, and one thing alone:
كان للبرنيمه معنى واحد فقط:

"In his house at R'lyeh dead Cthulhu waits dreaming."

"فن مرله فن رليه، يسطر كانولو الميت حالمًا".

Only two of the prisoners were found sane enough to be hanged.

لم يَعبر إلا على انيس من السجناء يبمعان بالعمل الكافن ليبم سمهما.

The rest of them were committed to various institutions.

أما البميه فقد نم إيداعهم فن موسسات محللمه.

All denied to have taken any part in the ritual murders.

ونفى الجميع مساركهم فن جرائم القبل الطقوسيه.

They said the killing had been done by something else.

قالوا إن عمليه القبل ارنكبت بواسطه سنء آخر.

"The black-winged ones," the each insisted, separately.

"دوى الاجنحه السوداء"، أصر كل مهم على حده.

They had come to them from their immemorial meeting-place.

لقد أنوا إليهم من مكان اجبماعهم القديم.

They had arisen out from the haunted woodlands.

لقد حرجوا من الغاباب المسكونه.

But the stories of mysterious allies were inconsistent.

لكن قصص الحلفاء الغامضين كانب مضاربه.

***

What the police did extract came mainly from one man.

ما اسحلصه السرطه جاء فن الغالب من رجل واحد.

An immensely aged mestizo named Castro.

رجل مسيسو مسقدم فن السن للغايه يدعى كاسرو.

He claimed to have sailed to strange ports.

وادعى أنه أبحر إلى موانى عريبه.

And he said he had been to the mountains of China.

وقال إنه رار جبال الصين.

There he talked with undying leaders of the cult.

وهناك بحدب مع قاده الطائفه الحالدين.

Old Castro remembered bits of hideous legend.

تذكر كاسرو العجوز أجزاء من أسطوره بسعه.

His legends paled the speculations of theosophists.

لقد فاقت أساطيره تكهنات المتصوفه.

His stories made man seem like a recent creation.

جعلت قصصه الإنسان يبدو وكأنه مخلوق حديث العهد.

Even the world was transient in his account of things.

حتى العالم كان عابراً في وصفه للامور.

There had been eons when other Things ruled on the earth.

لقد مرت دهور طويله كانت فيها أشياء أخرى تحكم الارض.

And they had had great cities here on the earth.

وكان لديهم مدن عظيمه هنا على الارض.

The deathless Chinamen told him reserved secrets.

أخبره الصينيون الخالدون بأسرار دفينه.

He had told him their ruins could still be found.

أخبره أنه لا يزال من الممكن العثور على آثارهم.

There were still Cyclopean stones on islands in the Pacific.

كان لا يزال هناك أحجار عملاقه على جزر في المحيط الهادى.

They all died vast epochs of time before man came.

لقد ماتوا جميعاً قبل ظهور الإنسان بعصور زمنيه طويله.

But there were knowledges and practices in ancients arts.

لكن كان هناك معارف وممارسات في الفنون القديمه.

Special rituals which could revive them again, in time.

طقوس خاصه يمكن أن تعيدهم إلى الحياه مره أخرى، مع مرور الوقت.

In the cycle of eternity their return was inevitable.

في دوره الأبديه، كان عودتهم أمراً لا مفر منه.

When the stars come round again to the right positions

عندما تعود النجوم إلى مواقعها الصحيحه

They had, indeed themselves come from the stars.

لقد أتوا هم أنفسهم من النجوم.

"These great old ones," Castro continued.

وتابع كاسرو قائلاً: "هؤلاء العظماء القدماء."

They were not composed entirely of flesh and blood.

لم تكن مولفة بالكامل من اللحم والدم.

They had shape," Castro insisted, confidently.

"كان لها سكل"، أصر كاسرو بثقه.

And he had strange proof for what he believed.

وكان لديه دليل عريب على ما كان يومن به.

But the shape they took on was not made of matter.

لكن السكل الذي اتخدوه لم يكن مصنوعاً من الماده.

When the stars were in their right positions.

عندما كانت النجوم فن مواقعها الصحيحه.

Then they could plunge from one world to another.

ثم يمكنهم الاسقال من عالم إلى آحر.

Because they can move themselves through the sky.

لأنها تستطيع أن تتحرك عبر السماء.

But when the stars were wrong, they cannot live.

لكن عندما تخطى النجوم، لا يمكنهم العيس.

And it is true that they no longer live like we do.

والحقيقه أنهم لم يعودوا يعيسون كما نعيس نحن.

But despite that, they never really die either.

لكن على الرعم من دلك، فإنهم لا يموتون حقا أيضا.

They rest in stone houses in their great city of R'lyeh.

يستقرون فن بيوت حجريه فن مديتهم العطيمه رليه.

They are preserved by the spells of mighty Cthulhu.

لقد حقظت هده الاسياء بفصل تعاويد كتولو العطيم.

So there they lie, unaffected by the passing of time.

وهكذا يرقدون هناك، عير مأترين بمرور الرمن.

And they wait for another glorious resurrection.

وهم يسطرون قيامه مجيده أحرى.

When the stars and earth are ready for them again.

عندما تكون النجوم والارص مستعده لهم مره أخرى.

But they are still dependent on an outside force.

لكنهم ما رالوا يعتمدون على قوه حارجيه.

A force from outside served to liberate their bodies.

لقد ساهمت قوه خارجيه فن تحرير أجسادهم.

The spells preserved them and kept them intact.

حفظتهم التعاويد وأبقتهم سليمين.

But the spells also kept them from breaking free.

لكن التعاويد منعتهم أيضاً من التحرر.

So they could only lie awake in the dark and think.

لذا لم يكن بوسعهم إلا أن يسلقوا مستيقطين فن الظلام ويفكروا.

***

In the meantime uncounted millions of years rolled by.

وفن عصون دلك، مرت ملايين السين التن لا تعد ولا تحصى.

They knew all that was occurring in the universe.

كانوا يعلمون بكل ما يحدث فن الكون.

Because their mode of speech was transmitted thought.

لأن طريقه كلامهم كانت تعتمد على نقل الافكار.

Even now they were talking in their tombs.

حتى الآن كانوا يتحدثون فن قبورهم.

Then, after infinities of chaos, the first men came.

ثم، بعد فوضى لا متاهيه، جاء الرجال الاوائل.

The great old ones spoke to the sensitive among them.

تحدث السيوح العظماء إلى دوى الحساسيه بينهم.

They spoke to them by molding their dreams.

لقد خاطبوهم من خلال تسكيل أحلامهم.

Only that way could their language reach the fleshly minds
of mammals.

بهذه الطريقه فقط يمكن للعتهم أن تصل إلى عقول الثدييات الجسديه.

Then, whispered Castro, those first men formed the cult.

ثم همس كاسرو قائلا: "هؤلاء الرجال الاوائل هم من سكلوا الطائفه."

They organized themselves around small idols.

لقد نظموا أنفسهم حول أصنام صغيره.

The small idols which the great ones had shown them.

الأصنام الصغيره التى أراها لهم العظماء.

Idols brought from dim eras from dark stars.

أصنام جُلبت من عصور حالكه من نجوم مظلمه.

That cult would never die till the stars came right again.

لن تموت تلك الطائفه حتى تعود النجوم إلى وضعها الطبيعى مره أخرى.

The secret priests were going to take great Cthulhu from His tomb.

كان الكهنه السريون يعتزمون إخراج تمثال كولو العظيم من قبره.

And they were going to revive His subjects.

وكانوا ينووون إحياء رعاياه.

And then Cthulhu was going to resume His rule of earth.

ثم كان كاثولو سيستأنف حكمه للارض.

The right time was going to reveal itself quite clearly.

سيتضح الوقت المناسب بشكل جلى.

At that time mankind will have become as the great old ones.

فى ذلك الوقت، سيصبح البشر مثل الكائنات القديمه العظيمه.

They will be free and wild and beyond good and evil.

سيكونون أحراراً وبريين، وسيتجاوزون الخير والشر.

Laws and morals are going to be thrown aside.

سيتم تجاهل القوانين والاخلاق.

All men will be shouting and killing and reveling in joy.

سيصرخ جميع الرجال ويقتلون ويمرحون فرحاً عظيماً.

Then the liberated old ones will teach them the new ways.

ثم سيعلمهم القدماء المحررون الطرق الجديده.

New ways to shout and kill and revel and enjoy.

طرق جديده للصراخ والقتل والاحتفال والاستمتاع.

And all the earth will flame with a holocaust of ecstasy and freedom.

وستشتعل الأرض كلها بمحرقه من النشوه والحريه.

Meanwhile the cult had to practice the appropriate rites.

وفى الوقت نفسه، كان على الطائفه ممارسه الطقوس المناسبه.

They had to keep alive the memory of those ancient ways.

كان عليهم الحفاظ على ذكرى تلك العادات القديمه.

And they had to shadow forth the prophecy of their return.
وكان عليهم أن يجسدوا نبوءه عودتهم.

In the elder time chosen men spoke with the entombed Old Ones.
فى الزمن القديم، كان الرجال المختارون يتحدثون مع الكائنات القديمه المدفونه.

The entombed Old Ones spoke to them in their dreams.
تحدث إليهم الكائنات القديمه المدفونه فى أحلامهم.

But then something disturbed their means of communication.
لكن بعد ذلك حدث سىء ما أدى إلى تعطيل وسائل اتصالهم.

The great stone in the city R'lyeh had sunk beneath the waves.
الحجر العظيم فى مدينه رليه تحت الأمواج.

And the monoliths and sepulchers were beneath the waters.
وكانت الصخور الضخمه والمقابر تحت المياه.

Deep waters full of the one primal mystery.
مياه عميقه مليئه بالسر البدائى الواحد.

Waters through which not even thought can pass.
مياه لا يمكن حتى للفكر أن يمر عبرها.

Water that cut off their spectral communication.
الماء الذى قطع اتصالهم الطيفى.

But the memory of the rites and rituals never died.
لكن ذكرى الطقوس والشعائر لم تموت أبداً.

And high priests said that the city would rise again.
وقال رؤساء الكهنه إن المدينه ستنهض من جديد.

When the stars were right Cthulhu was going to return.
عندما تكون الظروف مواتيه، سيعود كاثولو.

The moldy black spirits of the earth will come out again.
سعود الارواح السوداء المتعفنه للارض مره أخرى.

Shadowy black spirits full of dim rumors.
أرواح سوداء غامضه مليئه بالشائعات الخافته.

***

The spirits collected in caverns beneath forgotten sea-bottoms.

تجمعت الأرواح فى الكهوف الواقعه تحت قيعان البحار المنسيه.

But of those spirits old Castro dared not speak much.

لكن كاسرو العجوز لم يجرو على التحدث كثيراً عن تلك الارواح.

And he hurriedly cut himself off from the topic.

ثم قطع حديثه عن الموضوع على عجل.

No amount of persuasion could elicit more in this direction.

مهما بلغت محاولات الإقناع، فلن تجدى نفعاً فى تحقيق المزيد فى هذا الاتجاه.

No subtlety could convince him to speak of those spirits.

لم يكن لأى تلميح أن يقنعه بالحديث عن تلك الارواح.

The size of the old ones, too, he curiously declined to mention.

كما رفض بسكل غريب ذكر حجم القطع القديمه أيضاً.

And of the cult he spoke very little too.

ولم يتحدث كثيراً عن الطائفه أيضاً.

He thought the center lay amid the pathless deserts of Arabia.

كان يعتقد أن المركز يقع وسط صحارى الجزيره العربيه الشاسعه التى لا مسالك فيها.

There in Irem, the City of Pillars, dreams hidden and untouched.

هناك فى إيريم، مدينه الأعمده، الأحلام مخفيه ولم تمسها يد الإنسان.

This cult was not allied to the European witch-cult.

لم تكن هذه الطائفه متحالفه مع طائفه السحره الاوروبيه.

And the cult was virtually unknown beyond its members.

وكانت الطائفه غير معروفه تقريباً خارج نطاق أعصائها.

No book had ever really hinted of their knowledge.

لم يلمح أى كتاب قط إلى معرفتهم.

Though the deathless Chinamen said the mad Arab Abdul Alhazred came close.

على الرعم من أن الصيبيين الحالدين قالوا إن العربن المجنون عبد الحررد كان قريباً من دلك.

He said that there were double meanings in his Necronomicon.

وقال إن هناك معاني مردوجه فن كتابه "نيكرونوميكون."

The initiated were free to read it if they wanted to.

كان بإمكان المطلعين قراءته إدا رعبوا فن دلك.

And they should pay attention to one couplet in particular.

ويسبعن عليهم أن يولوا اهتماماً حاصاً لبيت سعرى واحد.

"That which is not dead can sleep for eternity,"

"ما لم يمت يمكنه أن ينام إلى الابد."

"And with strange eons even death may die."

"وحى الموت قد يموت مع مرور الدهور العريبه.".

Legrasse had been deeply impressed by what he heard.

ليعراس بسده بما سمعه.

And he was not a little bewildered by the tale.

وقد أنارت هده الحكايه حيره كبيره لديه.

He inquired in vain about the historic affiliations of the cult.

استقسر عبثاً عن الاسماءات الناريحيه للطائفه.

Castro, apparently, had told the truth about the oath of secrecy.

ويبدو أن كاسرو قد قال الحقيقه بسأن قسم السريه.

The authorities at Tulane University could not offer much help either.

لم سمكن السلطات فن جامعه نوليس من نقديم الكثير من المساعده أيضاً.

The were not able to shed no light upon neither cult, nor the image.

لم يتمكنوا من إلقاء أى صوء على الطائمه أو الصوره.

And now the detective had come to the highest authorities in the country.

والآن وصل المحقق إلى أعلى السلطات فن البلاد.

And he heard none other than Professor Webb' tale in Greenland.

وسمع قصه البروفيسور ويب فى جريلاند.

***

Legrasse's tale aroused feverish interest at the meeting.
ليعراس اهتماماً محموماً فى الاجتماع.

The story was not only significant in its implications.
لم تكن القصه مهمه فقط من حيث دلالاتها.

But the story was also corroborated by the statuette.
لكن القصه تم تأكيدها أيضاً من خلال التمثال الصغير.

The excitement echoed in the subsequent correspondence.
وقد انعكس هذا الحماس فى المراسلات اللاحقه.

Those who attended stayed in close contact with each other.
حافظ الحاضرون على تواصل وثيق فيما بينهم.

Although scant mention occurs in the formal publications.
على الرغم من قله ذكرها فى المنسورات الرسميه.

Caution is the first care of those accustomed to charlatanry.
الحذر هو أول ما يوحاه من اعتادوا على الدجل.

Impostures are kept out as much as it is possible.
يتم استبعاد المحتالين قدر الإمكان.

Legrasse for some time lent the image to Professor Webb.
ليعراس الصوره للبروفيسور ويب لبعض الوقت.

But at the latter's death the image was returned to him.
لكن عند وفاه الأخير، أعيدت الصوره إليه.

And the image remains in Legrasse's possession.
ولا تزال الصوره بحوزه ليعراس.

This is where I viewed the terrible image not long ago.
هذا هو المكان الذى شاهدت فيه تلك الصوره المروعه منذ وقت ليس ببعيد.

The image is unmistakably akin to Wilcox' dream-sculpture.
الصوره نسبه بسكل لا لبس فيه منحوته ويلكوكس الحالمه.

It was no wonder my uncle was so excited by his tale.
لم يكن من المستغرب أن يكون عمى متحمساً جداً لقصته.

- 58 -

And I'm not surprised he made the efforts he made.

ولا أستغرب الجهود التي بذلها.

He had heard everything Legrasse knew of the cult.

لقد سمع كل ما يعرفه ليغراس عن الطائفه.

And the strange cultish dreams of a sensitive young man.

والأحلام الغريبه الشبيهه بأحلام الطوائف التي تراود شابا حساسا.

The bas-relief just like the one from the swamp.

النقس البارز يشبه تماماً ذلك الموجود في المستنقع.

The addition of the devil tablet in Greenland.

إضافه لوح الشيطان في جرينلاند.

The exact same words used in three remote occurrences.

استخدمت نفس الكلمات بالضبط في ثلاث مناسبات متباعده.

The Eskimo diabolists, the mongrels in Louisiana, and then Wilcox.

عبده الشيطان من الإسكيمو، والأوغاد في لويزيانا، ثم ويلكوكس.

What other conclusion could one possibly have come to?

ما هي النتيجه الأخرى التي كان من الممكن التوصل إليها؟

It's only natural Professor Angel pursued this conclusion.

من الطبيعي أن يسعى البروفيسور أنجيل إلى التوصل إلى هذا الاستنتاج.

And I wouldn't have expected him to be less thorough.

ولم أكن أتوقع منه أن يكون أقل دقه.

My great-uncle was a man of principled academic rigor.

كان عمي الأكبر رجلا ذا مبادئ أكاديميه صارمه.

Though privately I also had other plausible theories.

مع ذلك، كانت لدي نظريات أخرى معقوله في قراره نفسي.

I suspected young Wilcox of having heard of the cult.

كنت أشك في أن الشاب ويلكوكس قد سمع عن الطائفه.

Maybe he had heard of the cult in some indirect way...

ربما كان قد سمع عن الطائفه بطريقه غير مباشره.

He could easily have invented a series of dreams.

كان بإمكانه بسهوله أن يخترع سلسله من الأحلام.

That way he could heighten and continue the mystery.

وبهذه الطريقه كان بإمكانه زياده الغموض واستمراره.

The dream-narratives and cuttings collected did of course corroborate..

وبالطبع، أكدت روايات الأحلام والمقاطع التي تم جمعها هذه النتائج.

But the rationalism of my mind had not yet been satisfied.

لكن عقلانيتي لم تكن قد اطمأنت بعد.

Coincidences can form highly believable illusions too.

يمكن أن تشكل المصادفات أوهاماً سديده التصديق أيضاً.

And we have to bear in mind the extravagance of the whole subject.

وعلينا أن نضع في اعتبارنا إسراف الموضوع برمته.

So I was led to adopt what I thought the most sensible conclusions.

لذلك دفعتني الظروف إلى تبني ما اعتقدت أنه الاستنتاجات الأكثر منطقيه.

I thoroughly studied the manuscript from the beginning.

لقد درست المخطوطه بدقه منذ البدايه.

And I correlated the theosophical and anthropological notes.

وقمت بربط الملاحظات اليوصوفيه والانثروبولوجيه.

I compared the literature with the cult narrative of Legrasse...

قارنت الادب بالسرديه الطائفيه لليغراس.

I made a trip to Providence to see the sculptor.

قمت برحله إلى بروفيدنس لرؤيه النحات.

And I intended to give him the rebuke I thought proper.

وكنت أنوي أن أوبخه بالاسلوب الذي أراه مناسباً.

There must be consequences, I felt, for the trick he played.

شعرت أنه لا بد من وجود عواقب للحيله التي دبرها.

He had boldly imposed himself upon a learned and aged man.

لقد فرض نفسه بجرأه على رجل متعلم وكبير في السن.

***

Wilcox still lived alone where my uncle had met him.

كان ويلكوكس لا يزال يعيش وحيداً في المكان الذي التقى به فيه عمي.

In the Fleur-de-Lys Building in Thomas Street.
فى مبنى زهره الزنبق فى سارع توماس.

A hideous Victorian imitation of Seventeenth Century
Breton architecture.
تقليد بشع على الطراز الفيكتورى للعماره البريتونيه فى القرن السابع عشر.

The building flaunted its stuccoed front amidst its
surroundings.
كان المبنى يباهى بواجهته المطليه بالجص وسط محيطه.

There were lovely Colonial houses on the ancient hill.
كانت هناك منازل استعماريه جميله على التل القديم.

And the house stood under the shadow of the finest
Georgian steeple in America.
وكان المنزل يقع تحت ظل أجمل برج جورجى فى أمريكا.

I found him at work in his rooms, among his sculptures.
وجدته منهمكاً فى عمله فى غرفه، بين منحوتاته.

The specimens scattered came from a very unique mind.
العينات المنثوره ناتج عقل فريد للغايه.

At once I conceded that his genius is indeed profound and
authentic.
أقررت على الفور بأن عبقريته عميقه وأصيله بالفعل.

He has crystallized in clay that which Arthur Machen evokes
in prose.
لقد جسد فى الطين ما يستحضره آرثر ماكين فى نثره.

He mirrored in marble the nightmares Clark Ashton Smith
put to canvas.
لقد عكس فى الرخام الكوابيس التى رسمها كلارك أشتون سميث على القماش.

He will, I believe, be spoken of one day as one of the great
decadents.
أعتقد أنه سيذكر يوماً ما كواحد من أعظم المنحرفين.

He was dark, frail, and somewhat unkempt in aspect.
كان أسمر البشره، نحيلا، ومظهره مهملا بعض الشىء.

He turned languidly at my knock on his door.
استدار بكسل عندما طرقت بابه.

He didn't rise from his seat when I came in.

لم يهض من مقعده عندما دخلت.

And he asked me what the purpose of my visit was.

وسألني عن الغرض من زيارتي.

When I told him who I was his interest was piqued.

عندما أخبرته من أنا، ازداد اهتمامه.

My uncle had excited his curiosity by probing his strange dreams.

أثار عمي فضوله من خلال اسكساف أحلامه الغريبه.

Although he had never explained the reason for the study.

على الرغم من أنه لم يوصح قط سبب إجراء الدراسه.

I did not enlarge his knowledge in this regard.

لم أساهم في زياده معرفه في هذا الساى.

But I sought with some subtlety to gain his confidence.

لكني سعيت، ببعض الدهاء، إلى كسب نقه.

In a short time I became convinced of his absolute sincerity.

وبعد فتره وجيزه، اقتنعت تماماً بصدقه المطلق.

He spoke of the dreams in a manner none could mistake.

تحدب عن الاحلام بطريقه لا يمكن لاحد أن يحطى فيها.

His dreams' subconscious residuum had influenced his art profoundly.

لقد أثرت بقايا أحلامه اللاواعيه بسكل عميق على فه.

He showed me a morbid statue of the likes I had never seen before.

أراني نمالاً كىباً لم أَر مثله من قبل.

The statue's contours almost made me shake with fear.

كادت ملامح التمثال أن تجعلني أرتجف من الحوف.

The potency of the statue's black suggestion was overbearing.

كانت قوه الإيحاء الأسود للتمثال طاعيه.

He could not recall having seen the original of this thing.

لم يسطع أن يتذكر أنه رأى النسحه الاصليه من هذا الستىء.

But the statue was inspired by his own dream bas-relief.

لكن المال أسلَهم من نفس بارر كان يحلم به.

The outlines had formed themselves insensibly under his hands.

نسكلب الحطوط العريصه بسكل غير محسوس نحب يديه.

It was, no doubt, the giant shape he had raved of in delirium.

لا سك أنه كان السكل العملاو الدى كان يهدئ به فن حاله الهديان.

That he really knew nothing of the hidden cult he soon made clear.

سرعان ما أوضح أنه لم يكن سيباً عن الطائفه السريه.

Only my uncle's relentless catechism had given him some clues,

لم يكن سوى نعليم عمن المواصل للمسيحيه هو ما أعطاه بعض الدلائل.

And again I strove to explain the obvious conclusions away.

ومره أحرى، سعيت جاهداً لنفسير الاسساجاب الواصحه ونبريرها.

How he could possibly have received the weird impressions?

كيف يَعمل أن يكون قد نلمى نلك الانطباعات العريبه؟

He talked of his dreams in a strangely poetic fashion.

نحدب عن أحلامه بأسلوب سعرى عريب.

He made me see with terrible vividness the vistas of his dream.

لقد جعلنى أرى بوصوح مروع ماطر حلمه.

The damp Cyclopean city of slimy green stone.

مديبه عملاقه رطبه داب حجر أحصر لرج.

The geometry he oddly said, was all wrong.

قال بسكل عريب إن الهدسه كانب حاطبه بماماً.

And he spoke of what he heard with frightened expectancy.

ونحدب عما سمعه برقب حائف.

The ceaseless, half-mental calling from underground:

الداء المواصل، سبه الجبوني، من نحب الارص:

"Cthulhu fhtagn... Cthulhu fhtagn"

"كـولو فـاجن ... كـولو فـاجن"

These words had formed part of that dreaded ritual.

لقد سكلب هده الكلماب جزءاً من بلك الطموس المرعبه.

The ritual the told of dead Cthulhu's dream-vigil.

الطموس البي روب حلم كمولو الميب - سهربه.

The ritual that told of his stone vault at R'lyeh.

الطموس البي بحدب عن قبو الحجر الحاص به فى رليه.

And I felt deeply moved, despite my rational beliefs.

وسعرب بأبر عميو، على الرعم من معمدابى العملابيه.

Wilcox, I was sure, had heard of the cult in some casual way.

كب مأكدا من أن ويلكوكس قد سمع عن الطائفه بطريمه عابره.

He spent his time in a mass of equally weird literature.

لمد أمصى وقبه فى قراءه كم هائل من الادب العريب ببس المدر.

He must have forgotten the source of his knowledge.

لا بد أنه سبن مصدر معرفه.

Later the cult had found subconscious expression in his
dreams.

وفى وقب لاحو، وجدب الطائفه بعبيراً لا سعورياً فى أحلامه.

But this is natural when stories are so impressive.

لكن هدا أمر طبيعى عبدما بكون المصص مبيره للإعجاب إلى هدا الحد.

Finally the cult's ideas manifested themselves in the bas-
relief.

وأحيراً، بجلب أفكار الطائفه فى المعوس البارره.

And now the subject of the cult manifested itself in the
terrible statue.

والآن بجلى موصوع الطائفه فى الممال الرهيب.

I was convinced his imposture upon my uncle had been very
innocent.

كب مقبعاً بأن حداعه لعمى كان بريئاً بماماً.

He both slightly affected, and slightly ill-mannered.

كان مأبراً بعص السىء، وفليلا ما كان سيى الادب.

He had a disposition which I could never like.

كان يبمع بطباع لم أسطع أبداً أن أحبها.

But I was willing enough now to admit his genius.

لكنى كتب مسعداً الآن بما يكفى للاعتراف بعبقريه.

And I have no way of denying his honesty either.
وليس لدى أى وسيله لإنكار صدقه أيضاً.

Despite my initial feelings, I took leave of him amicably.
على الرغم من مساعرى الاوليه، فقد ودعته بود.

And I wish him all the success his talent promises.
وأتمنى له كل النجاح الذى تعد به موهبته.

***

The matter of the cult continued to fascinate me.
استمرت مسأله الطائفه فى إثاره اهتمامى.

At times I had visions of the personal fame I could attain.
فى بعض الاحيان كنت أرى رؤى للسهره الشخصيه التى يمكننى تحقيقها.

I visited New Orleans and talked with Legrasse.
زرت نيو أورليانز وتحدثت مع ليغراس.

And I spoke with other policemen of that swamp raid.
وتحدثت مع رجال شرطه آخرين بشأن مداهمه المستنقع تلك.

I saw the frightful image with my own eyes.
رأيت الصوره المرعبه بأم عينى.

And I even questioned some of the surviving mongrel prisoners.
بل إننى استجوبت بعض السجناء الهجناء الناجين.

Old Castro, unfortunately, had been dead for some years.
لسوء الحظ، كان كاسترو العجوز قد توفى منذ سنوات.

What I now heard so graphically at first hand excited me afresh.
ما سمعته الآن بوضوح شديد وبشكل مباشر أثارنى من جديد.

Though it was really no more than a detailed confirmation.
مع أنها لم تكن فى الحقيقه أكثر من مجرد تأكيد مفصل.

What they told me I had already read in my uncle's notes.
ما أخبرونى به كنت قد قرأته بالفعل فى مذكرات عمى.

I felt sure that I was on the track of a very real secret.

سعرت باليقين أني كنت على درب سر حقيقي للغايه.

And I was sure I was going to discover a very ancient religion.

وكنت متأكدًا من أني سأكسف ديانه قديمه جدًا.

The discovery would make me an anthropologist of note.

سيجعلني هذا الاكتساف عالم أنثروبولوجيا بارزاً.

My attitude was still one of absolute rational materialism.

كان موقفي لا يزال موقفاً قائماً على الماديه العقلانيه المطلقه.

And I wish my attitude to the subject matter had not changed.

وأتمنى لو لم يتغير موقفي تجاه هذا الموضوع.

I discounted with almost inexplicable perversity the coincidences.

تجاهلت هذه المصادفات بعناد يكاد يكون غير مبرر.

The dream notes and odd cuttings collected by Professor Angell.

ملاحظات الأحلام والقصاصات الغريبه التي جمعها البروفيسور أنجيل.

One thing I began to doubt was the cause of my uncle's death.

أحد الأمور التي بدأت أشك فيها هو سبب وفاه عمي.

I began to suspect his death was far from natural.

بدأت أشك في أن وفاته كانت بعيده كل البعد عن كونها طبيعيه.

And I now fear I know my uncle's death was not natural.

وأحسى الآن أني أعلم أن وفاه عمي لم تكن طبيعيه.

It was on a narrow hill street where he fell.

سقط في سارع ضيق على تله.

The street lead up from the ancient waterfront.

كان السارع يؤدي من الواجهه البحريه القديمه.

The port-town swarms with foreign mongrels.

تعج المدينه الساحليه بالكلاب الاجنبيه المختلطه.

He fell after a careless push from a negro sailor.

سقط بعد دفعه طائشه من بحار أسود.

I had not forgotten the mixed blood of the cult-members in Louisiana.

لم أنس الدم المختلط لأعضاء الطائفه في لويزيانا.

I had not forgotten the sailors in the voodoo orgy.

لم أنس البحاره في طقوس الفودو.

And would not be surprised to learn that they had other knowledge too.

ولن أفاجأ إذا علمت أن لديهم معارف أخرى أيضاً.

Secret methods as anciently known as the cryptic rites.

أساليب سريه تعرف قديماً بالطقوس الغامضه.

Poison needles as ruthless their demonic beliefs.

إبر مسمومه لا ترحم، تعكس معتقداتهم الشيطانيه.

Legrasse and his men, it is true, have been let alone.

ليغراس ورجاله قد تركوا وشأنهم.

But in Norway a certain seaman who saw things is dead.

لكن في النرويج، مات بحار كان يرى أشياء غريبه.

Might not sinister ears have picked up my uncle's interest in the sculptor?

ربما التقطت آذان خبيثه اهتمام عمي بالنحات؟

Might not the deeper inquiries of my uncle have drawn someone's attention?

ألا يمكن أن تكون استفسارات عمي المعمقه قد لفتت انتباه أحدهم؟

I think Professor Angell died because he knew too much.

أعتقد أن البروفيسور أنجيل مات لأنه كان يعرف الكثير.

Or he died because he was likely to learn too much.

أو ربما مات لأنه كان من المحتمل أن يتعلم الكثير.

Whether I shall go out as he did remains to be seen.

يبقى أن نرى ما إذا كنت سأرحل كما فعل هو.

Because I too have learned much about Cthulhu.

لأنني أنا أيضاً تعلمت الكثير عن كولو.

The Madness from the Sea
جنون البحر

There is one great boon heaven could grant me.

هناك نعمه عظيمه واحده يمكن أن يمنحنى إياها الله.

The total effacing of the results of a mere chance.

محو نام لنائج مجرد صدفه.

I wish I had never seen that stray piece of paper.

أتمنى لو لم أرَ تلك الورقه الضاله أبداً.

My daily routine would normally not have taken me there.

فى الظروف العاديه، لم يكن روتينى اليومى ليعودنى إلى هناك.

On any other day I would not have noticed anything.

فى أى يوم آخر، لم أكن لألاحظ أى شىء.

It was an old number of an Australian journal.

كان رقماً قديماً لمجله أستراليه.

The Sydney Bulletin for April 18, 1925

صحيفه سيدنى بوليسين، 18 أبريل 1925

The paper had even slipped past the cutting bureau.

بل إن الورقه قد أفلتت من مكتب القص.

I had largely given over my inquiries to a friend.

لقد أوكلت معظم استفساراتى إلى صديق.

He had taken on the work of most of the research.

لقد تولى معظم أعمال البحث.

He had come to refer to the group as the "Cthulhu Cult".

وقد أصبح يسير إلى المجموعه باسم "طائفه كثولو."

I was visiting my learned friend of Paterson, New Jersey.

كنت أزور صديقى المثقف فى باترسون، نيو جيرسى.

The curator of a local museum, and a mineralogist of note.

أمين متحف محلى، وعالم معادن بارز.

While at his museum I had access to the reserved specimens.

أثناء وجودى فى متحفه، أتيحت لى فرصه الاطلاع على العينات المحفوظه.

And this is when an odd picture caught my attention.

وهنا لفت انتباهي صوره غريبه.

Beneath one of the stones was the Sydney Bulletin I mentioned,

كان صحيفه "سيدني بوليس" التي ذكرتها موجوده أسفل أحد الاحجار.

My friend has wide affiliations in all conceivable foreign lands.

صديقي لديه علاقات واسعه في جميع البلدان الأجنبيه التي يمكن تصورها.

The picture was a half-tone cut of a hideous stone image.

كانت الصوره عباره عن نسخه نصفيه من صوره حجريه بشعه.

Almost identical with the stone Legrasse had found in the swamp.

يكاد يكون مطابقاً للحجر الذي عثر عليه ليغراس في المستنقع.

Eagerly I read the article for its precious contents.

قرأت المقال بشغف لما يحتويه من معلومات قيمه.

But I was disappointed to find that it was just a short article.

لكني شعرت بخيبه أمل عندما اكتشفت أنها مجرد مقاله قصيره.

Although brief, the information was of portentous significance.

على الرغم من إيجازها، إلا أن المعلومات كانت ذات أهميه بالغه.

***

"MYSTERY DERELICT FOUND AT SEA"

"العثور على سفينه مهجوره غامضه في البحر"

Vigilant Arrives With Helpless Armed New Zealand Yacht in Tow.

وصلت سفينه "فيجيلانت" وهي تجر يختًا نيوزيلنديًا مسلحًا عاجزًا.

One Survivor and one Dead Man Found Aboard.

تم العثور على ناج واحد ورجل ميت على متن السفينه.

Tale of Desperate Battle and Deaths at Sea.

قصه معركه يائسه ووفيات في البحر.

Rescued Seaman Refuses Particulars of Strange Experience.

البحار الذي تم إنقاذه يرفض الإدلاء بتفاصيل عن التجربه الغريبه.

Odd Idol Found in His Possession, Inquiry to Follow.
تم العثور على تمثال غريب بحوزته، وسيتم إجراء تحقيق لاحق.

The Alert of Dunedin yacht, N.Z., had been disabled in battle.
تم تعطيل اليخت "ألرت أوف دنيدن" التابع لسركه "إن زد" فى المعركه.

Previously the ship had left from Valparaiso on March 25th.
وكانت السفينه قد غادرت سابقاً من فالبارايسو فى 25 مارس.

On April 2nd the ship was driven considerably south of her course.
فى الثانى من أبريل، انحرفت السفينه بسكل كبير جنوب مسارها.

Exceptionally heavy storms had redirected the ship.
أدت عواصف سديده بسكل استثنائى إلى تغيير مسار السفينه.

Monster waves forced the ship to take a different route.
أجبرت الامواج الهائله السفينه على اتخاد مسار محتلف.

On April 12th the ship was sighted by another ship.
فى الثانى عسر من أبريل، رصدت سفينه أخرى السفينه.

Latitude 34° 21', Longitude 152° 17'
حط العرض 34° 21'، حط الطول 152° 17'

Initially they thought the ship had been deserted.
فى البدايه طنوا أن السفينه مهجوره.

But one still living man had been found on board.
لكن تم العثور على رجل واحد لا يزال على قيد الحياه على من السفينه.

This lone survivor was in a half-delirious condition.
كان هدا الناجى الوحيد فى حاله سبه هديان.

The only other victim found was a man already dead a week.
الضحيه الاخرى الوحيده التى تم العثور عليها كانت رجلا متوفى مد أسبوع.

Now the heavily armed steam yacht was being towed.
والآن يتم سحب اليخت البحارى المدجج بالسلاح.

And this morning the ship was coming in to its wharf.
وفى صباح هدا اليوم، كانت السفينه تدحل إلى رصيفها.

The living man was clutching a horrible stone idol.
كان الرجل الحى ممسكاً بتصم حجرى بسع.

The stone idol was about a foot in height.

كان ارتفاع الصنم الحجرى حوالى قدم.

And the origins of the stone were completely unknown.
وكان أصول الحجر مجهوله تماماً.

Authorities at Sydney university were baffled.
سعرت السلطات فى جامعه سيدنى بالحيره.

The Royal Society couldn't offer information about the idol.
لم تمكن الجمعيه الملكيه من تقديم معلومات عن الصنم.

And the Museum in College street had no insights either.
ولم يقدم المتحف الموجود فى سارع الكليه أى روى مفيده أيضاً.

The survivor says he found the stone in the cabin of the yacht.
يقول الناجى إنه عتر على الحجر فى مقصوره اليحت.

Allegedly the idol was in a small carved shrine.
ويزعم أن الصنم كان موجوداً فى صريح صعير مصحوب.

And the carvings of the shrine were of common pattern.
وكان نقوس الصريح ذات نمط سايع.

This man eventually recovered back to his senses.
اسعاد هذا الرجل وعيه فى نهايه المطاف.

And he told an exceedingly strange story of piracy and slaughter.
وروى قصه عريبه للعايه عن القرصنه والمذابح.

He is Gustaf Johansen, a Norwegian of some intelligence.
إنه عوساف يوهانس، وهو نرويجى يتمع ببعض الدكاء.

And he had been second mate of the two-masted schooner Emma of Auckland.
وكان يسعل منصب الصابط الثانى على من السفينه السراعيه ذات الصاريين "إيما" التابعه لأوكلاند.

The ship sailed for Callao February 20th, manned by eleven sailors.
أبحرت السفينه إلى كالاو فى 20 فبراير، وعلى منها أحد عسر بحاراً.

The ship, he says, was delayed and thrown widely south of her course.
ويقول إن السفينه تأخرت وانحرفت جنوب مسارها بسكل كبير.

There was a great storm on March 1st, and on March 22nd.

هب عاصفه سديده فى الاول من مارس، وفى الثانى والعسرين من مارس.

On their journey they encountered another ship.

وفى رحلتهم صادفوا سفينه أخرى.

This was in S. Latitude 49° 51′, W. Longitude 128° 34′

كان هدا فى حط عرض جنوبى 49° 51′، وحط طول غربى 128° 34′

This ship was manned by a queer and evil-looking crew.

كانت هذه السفينه تدار من قبل طاقم غريب الاطوار ودو مطهر سرير.

All the men were of Kanakas and half-castes.

كان جميع الرجال من الكاناكا ومن دوى الاصول المحتلطه.

Being ordered peremptorily to turn back, Capt. Collins refused.

رفض الكابتن كولينز العوده بعد أن أمر بدلك بسكل قاطع.

Without warning the strange crew began to shoot savagely upon the schooner.

وبدون سابق إندار، بدأ الطاقم الغريب بإطلاق النار بوحسيه على السفينه السراعيه.

They shot a peculiarly heavy battery of brass cannon.

أطلموا وابلا تقيلا بسكل غريب من المدافع النحاسيه.

The men from his ship showed fighting spirit, says the survivor.

ويقول الناجن إن الرجال الذين كانوا على من سفينه أطهروا روحاً قتاليه.

The schooner began to sink from shots beneath the waterline.

بدأت السفينه السراعيه بالغرق من الطلقات التى تلقاها أسفل حط الماء.

But they managed to heave alongside their enemy boat, and board her.

لكنهم تمكنوا من الالتفاف بجانب قارب العدو والصعود على متنه.

They grappled with the savage crew on the yacht's deck.

اسبكوا مع الطاقم المتوحس على سطح اليحت.

Their mode of fighting seemed to be strangely clumsy.

بدا أسلوب قتالهم غريباً وغير متقن.

But defeat did not seem to be an option for these savage men.

لكن الهزيمه لم نكن حياراً مطروحاً أمام هولاء الرجال المـوحسـيـن.

They had a particularly abhorrent and desperate way of fighting.

كان لديهم أسلوب قـال بعيص ويأس بسكل حاص.

So they had no choice but to kill all men of the enemy ship..

لدلك لم يكن أمامهم حيار سوى فـل جميع رجال سفيـه العدو.

Three of their men were also killed in the fight.

كما قُـل نلانه من رجالهم فن المعركه.

Capt. Collins and First Mate Green were among the dead.

كان الكابس كوليـر والصابط الاول عريس من بين الفـلى.

Second Mate Johansen took over control from First Mate Green.

نولى الصابط الـانى يوهانس رمام الأمور من الصابط الأول عريس.

And the remaining eight men proceeded to navigate the captured yacht.

وسرع الرجال الـمانيه الـسبعون فـن قياده اليحـت الدى نم الاسـيلاء عليه.

They proceeded to continue in the original direction they were going.

نم واصلوا السير فـن الانجاه الأصلـن الدى كانوا يسيرون فيه.

To see if there had been any reason they were ordered to turn around.

للـأكد مما إذا كان هناك أى سبب لأمرهم بالعوده.

***

The next day, it appears, they landed on a small island.

وفـن اليوم الـالـن، على ما يبدو، هبطوا على جريره صعيره.

Although no island is known to exist in that part of the ocean.

على الرعم من أنه لا نوجد جريره معروفه فـن دلك الجرء من المحيط.

Six of the men somehow died ashore while on the island.

توفن سه من الرجال بطريقه ما على الساطى أساء وجودهم على الجريره.

Though Johansen is queerly reticent about this part of his
story.
على الرعم من أن يوهانس محفظ بسكل عريب بسأن هذا الجزء من قصه.

And he speaks only of their falling into a rock chasm.
وهو لا يحدب إلا عن سموطهم فن هوه صحريه.

Later, it seems, he and one companion boarded the yacht.
وفن وقب لاحو، يبدو أنه وأحد رفاقه صعدا على من اليحب.

Together they tried to sail the ship, undermanned.
حاولوا معاً الإبحار بالسفيبه، رعم فله عدد أفراد الطافم.

But they were beaten about by the storm of April 2nd.
لكن عاصفه الثانن من أبريل حطمهم.

From that time till his rescue on the 12th, the man
remembers little.
مذ ذلك الوقب وحبى إنعاده فن الثانن عسر من السهر، لا يذكر الرجل سوى
القليل.

And he does not even recall when William Briden, his
companion, died.
وهو لا يبدكر حبى مبى نوفن ويليام برايدن، رفيمه.

Autopsy could reveal no obvious cause to Briden's death.
لم يكسف بسريح الجبه عن سبب واصح لوفاه بريدن.

The most likely cause of death is exposure to the elements.
السبب الاكبر برجيحاً للوفاه هو البعرص للعوامل الجويه.

The Dunedin reported that their boat, the Alert, was well
known.
ذكرب صحيفه "دا ديدن" أن قاربهم، المسمى "أليرب"، كان معروفاً جيداً.

The island traders bore an evil reputation along the
waterfront.
كان لبجار الجريره سمعه سيبه على طول الواجهه البحريه.

The ship was owned by a curious group of half-castes.
كانب السفيبه مملوكه لمجموعه عريبه من دوئ الاصول المحبلطه.

Frequent meetings and night trips to the woods attracted
curiosity.

أنارب الاجماعات المسكرره والرحلات الليليه إلى العابه فصول الناس.

The ship had set sail in great haste on March 1st.
أبحرب السفيه على عجل كبير فن الاول من مارس.

Just after the storm, and the earth tremors that night.
بعد العاصفه مباسره، اهـرب الارص فن بلك الليله.

Our Auckland correspondent gives the Emma excellent reputation.
مراسلنا فن أوكلاند يمبح إيما سمعه ممساره.

The Crew from the Emma were held very in high regard.
كان طاقم سفيه إيما يحطى بـمدير كبير.

And Johansen is described as a sober and worthy man.
ويوصف يوهانس بأنه رجل رزين وجدير بالـمه.

The admiralty will institute an inquiry on the whole matter.
سجرى الاميراليه بحميماً فن المسأله برمها.

Starting tomorrow they will collect all relevant information.
ابـداء من العد، سيهومون بجمع جميع المعلومات داب الصله.

Every effort will be made to induce Johansen to speak.
سيبم بدل كل جهد ممكن لحب جوهاسس على الكلام.

This and the hellish image were all the information I had to go on.
هدا بالإصافه إلى الصوره المروعه كانا كل المعلومات البن كانب لدى لأعـمد عليها.

But what a train of ideas that little information started in my mind!
لكن يا لها من سلسله أفكار أنارها بلك المعلومه البسيطه فن دهـن!

Here were new treasuries of data on the Cthulhu Cult.
ها كانب هناك كـور جديده من البيابات حول طائفه كـولو.

The cult not only had interests on land.
لم بـمصر مصالح الطائمه على الارص فحسب.

Now there was evidence they also had connections to the sea.
والآن، ظهرب أدله على أن لديهم أيضاً صلات بالبحر.

What motive prompted the hybrid crew to order back the Emma?

ما الدافع الذى دفع الطاقم الهجين إلى إصدار أمر بإعادة سفينه إيما؟

Why did they sail about with their hideous idol?

لماذا كانوا يبحرون حاملين صنمهم البشع؟

What was the unknown island on which six of the Emma's crew had died?

ما هى الجزيره المجهوله التى مات عليها سته من أفراد طاقم إيما؟

And why was Johansen so secretive about their death?

ولماذا كان يوهانس مكتما للعايه بشأن وفاتهم؟

What had the vice-admiralty's investigation brought out?

ما الذى كسف عنه تحقيق نائب الاميراليه؟

And what was known of the noxious cult in Dunedin?

وماذا كان معروفاً عن الطائفه الضاره فى ديدن؟

Nor could one help but marvel at the timing of the events.

ولا يسع المرء إلا أن يتعجب من توقيت الاحداث.

There was a deep and more than natural linkage between the dates.

كان هناك ارتباط عميق وطبيعى للعايه بين التواريح.

A malign and now undeniable significance to the various turns of events.

أهميه حبيثه لا يمكن إنكارها الآن لمختلف منعطفات الأحداث.

***

My uncle had noted with great care the connecting events.

لاحط عمى بعنايه فائمه الاحداث المترابطه.

On March 1st the earthquake and storm had come.

فى الأول من مارس، وقع الزلزال والعاصفه.

February 28th, according to the International Date Line.

28 فبراير، وفما لحط التاريح الدولى.

From Dunedin the noisome crew of the Alert darted eagerly forth.

انطلق طاقم سفينه "ألرت" المزعج من مديه ديدن بحماس سديد.

They moved as if they had been imperiously summoned.

نحركوا كما لو أنهم اسدعوا بأمرٍ قاطع.

On the other side of the earth the other events unfolded.
وعلى الجانب الآخر من الأرض، وقعت أحداث أخرى.

Poets and artists had begun to have their strange dreams.
بدأ السعراء والفانون يروں أحلامهم العريبه.

Dreams of a dank Cyclopean city from times long gone.
أحلام مديبه عملاقه رطبه من أرمسه عابره.

A young sculptor was persuaded by these dreams too.
وقد أقىعب هده الاحلام ىحاىا سابا أيصا.

In his sleep he molded the form of the dreaded Cthulhu.
فى ىومه، قام بسكيل هيبه كىولو المرعب.

On March 23rd the crew of the Emma landed on an
unknown island.
فى 23 مارس، هبط طاقم سفيبه إيما على جريره مجهوله.

There on that island they left six men dead.
هماك على ىلك الجريره ىركوا سه رجال فىلى.

On that date the dreams of sensitive men assumed a
heightened vividness.
فى دلك الباريح، اىحدث أحلام الرجال الحساسيں وصوحاً مرايداً.

Their dreams darkened with dread of a giant monster's
malign pursuit.
أطلمت أحلامهم برعب من مطارده وحس عملاق سريره.

One architect went mad from his dreams that night.
أصيب أحد المهىدسيں المعماريىں بالجىوں بسبب أحلامه فى ىلك الليله.

And a sculptor had lapsed suddenly into delirium!
وفجأه، دحل ىحاب فى حاله هدياں!

And then there was the storm of April 2nd.
ىم جاءت عاصفه الباىى من أبريل.

The date on which all dreams of the dank city ceased.
الباريح الدى اسهت فيه كل أحلام المديبه الكىيبه.

Wilcox emerged unharmed from the bondage of strange
fever.
حرج ويلكوكس سالماً من براں الحمى العريبه.

And everything appeared to be normal again.

وبدا كل سىء طبيعياً مره أحرى.

But what about the hints old Castro had suggested?

لكن مادا عن التلميحات التى أشار إليها كاسرو العجور؟

What about the sunken, star-born old ones?

ومادا عن الكائنات القديمه العارفه، المولوده من النجوم؟

What about their promised return and coming reign?

ومادا عن عودتهم الموعوده وحكمهم القادم؟

What about their faithful cult and their mastery of dreams?

ومادا عن طائفتهم المخلصه وإتقانهم للاحلام؟

Was I tottering on the brink of cosmic horrors?

هل كنت أترجح على حافه أهوال كونيه؟

Cosmic horrors far beyond man's power to bear?

أهوال كونيه تفوق قدره الإنسان على تحملها؟

If so, they must be horrors of the mind alone.

إذا كان الأمر كذلك، فلا بد أنها مجرد أهوال عقليه.

On the second of April there was sudden coordinated calm.

فى الثانى من أبريل، ساد هدوء مفاجى ومنسق.

The monstrous menace that sieged mankind's soul had vanished.

لقد اختفى الخطر الوحشى الذى حاصر روح البشريه.

That evening I made all necessary arrangements for onwards travel.

فى ذلك المساء، قمت باتخاد جميع الترتيبات اللازمه لمواصله السفر.

I bade my host adieu and took a train for San Francisco.

ودعت مضيفى واستقليت القطار إلى سان فرانسيسكو.

***

In less than a month I was at the port of Dunedin.

فى أقل من شهر كنت فى ميناء دنيدن.

Here, however, my investigation stumbled slightly.

لكن هنا، نعثر نحميون قليلاً.

I inquired in the old sea taverns where the men had lingered.

استفسرت فن الحانات البحريه القديمه حيث كان الرجال يترددون عليها.

But little was known of the strange cult members.

لكن لم يكن معروفاً الكثير عن أعضاء الطائفه الغريبه.

Waterfront scum was far too common for special mention.

كانت الحثاله على الواجهه البحريه شائعه للغايه لدرجه لا تستدعن ذكرها بشكل خاص.

But there was vague talk about one inland trip these mongrels had made.

لكن كان هناك حديث مبهم عن رحله داخليه واحده قام بها هؤلاء الاوغاد.

Faint drumming and red flames were noted on the distant hills.

لوحظت أصوات طبول خافته وألسنه لهب حمراء على التلال البعيده.

In Auckland I learned only a little more of Johansen.

فن أوكلاند، لم أتعرف إلا على القليل من المعلومات الإضافيه عن يوهانسن.

He had been taken to Sydney for the investigation.

تم نقله إلى سيدنن لإجراء التحقيق.

A perfunctory and inconclusive questioning turned his hair white.

أدى الاستجواب السطحن وغير الحاسم إلى تحول شعره إلى اللون الأبيض.

Thereafter he sold his cottage in West Street.

وبعد ذلك باع كوخه فن شارع ويست.

And he sailed with his wife to his old home in Oslo.

وأبحر مع زوجته إلى منزله القديم فن أوسلو.

His experience had clearly stirred him deeply.

من الواضح أن تجربته قد أثرت فيه بعمق.

But he told his friends no more than he had told the admiralty officials.

لكنه لم يخبر أصدقاءه بأكثر مما أخبر به مسوولن الأميراليه.

And all they could do was to give me his Oslo address.

وكل ما استطاعوا فعله هو إعطائن عنوانه فن أوسلو.

After that I went to Sydney and talked profitlessly with seamen.

بعد ذلك ذهبت إلى سيدني وتحدثت مع البحاره دون جدوى.

Members of the vice-admiralty court could not enlighten me either.

لم يسطع أعضاء محكمه نائب الأميراليه أن يوضحوا لي الأمر أيضاً.

I tracked the Alert down to Circular Quay in Sydney Cove.

لقد تبعت مصدر الإندار إلى سيركولار كواي في سيدني كوف.

The ship had been sold and was again in commercial use.

تم بيع السفينه وعادت للاستخدام التجاري.

But I could gain no further clues from the ship's cargo.

لكني لم أتمكن من الحصول على أي أدله أخرى من حموله السفينه.

The image was preserved in the Museum at Hyde Park.

تم حفظ الصوره في متحف هايد بارك.

The cuttlefish head, dragon body, and scaly wings.

رأس الحبار، وجسم التنين، والاجنحه ذات الحراشف.

The monster crouching atop the hieroglyphed pedestal.

الوحش الجاثم فوق القاعده المنقوشه بالهيروغليفيه.

I studied every detail of the idol long and well.

لقد درست كل تفاصيل الصنم بدقه وبأن.

The relic was a thing of balefully exquisite workmanship.

كانت القطعه الاثريه تحفه فنيه رائعه بشكل مأساوي.

I couldn't help but notice the similarity to Legrasse's smaller specimen.

لم يسعني إلا أن ألاحظ التشابه مع عينه ليغراس الأصغر حجماً.

Both idols had the same utter mystery and terrible antiquity.

كان لكلا الصنمين نفس الغموص المطلق والقديم المروع.

And both idols had the same unearthly strangeness of material.

وكان لكلا الصنمين نفس الغرابه غير الأرضيه للماده.

Geologists, the curator told me, had found it a monstrous puzzle.

أخبرني أمين المتحف أن الجيولوجيين وجدوا الأمر لغزاً هائلاً.

They insisted that the world held no rock like this one.

أصروا على أنه لا يوجد فى العالم صخره مثل هذه.

Then I thought with a shudder of what old Castro had told Legrasse.

ثم فكرت بقشعريره فيما قاله كاسرو العجوز لليغراس.

The tale of the primal great ones, sunken under the sea.

قصه الكائنات العظيمه البدائيه، الغارقه تحت سطح البحر.

"They had come from the stars."

"لقد أتوا من النجوم".

"They had brought their images with them."

"لقد أحضروا صورهم معهم".

I was shaken with a mental revolution as I had never before known.

لقد اهترب بثوره فكريه لم أشهد مثلها من قبل.

I was now completely resolved to visit Mate Johansen in Oslo.

كنت الآن مصمماً تماماً على زياره مانت يوهانس فى أوسلو.

Sailing for London, I re-embarked at once for the Norwegian capital.

أبحرت إلى لندن، ثم عدت على الفور إلى العاصمه النرويجيه.

And one autumn day I landed at the wharves.

وفى أحد أيام الخريف، وصلت إلى الارصفه.

***

Johansen's hometown was in the shadow of the Egeberg.

كان مسقط رأس يوهانس يقع فى ظل إيغبرغ.

I discovered he lived in the Old Town of King Harold Haardrada.

اكتشفت أنه كان يعيش فى البلده القديمه للملك هارولد هاردرادا.

For centuries the greater city had masqueraded as "Christiania".

لعده قرون، تسترت المدينه الكبرى تحت اسم "كريستيانيا".

King Harald Hardrada kept alive the name of Oslo.

حافظ الملك هارالد هاردرادا على اسم أوسلو.

I made the brief trip to his residences by taxicab.

قمت برحله قصيره إلى مساكنه بواسطه سياره أجره.

A neat and ancient building with plastered front.

مبنى أنيق وقديم ذو واجهه مطليه بالجص.

And I knocked with palpitant heart at the door.

وطرقت الباب بقلب يخفق بسده.

A sad-faced woman in black answered my summons.

استجابت لندائي امرأه حزينه الوجه ترتدى ملابس سوداء.

I was stung with disappointment at the sight.

سعرت بخيبه أمل سديده عند رويه ذلك.

She told me in halting English that Gustaf Johansen was no more.

أخبرتني بلغه إنجليزيه متقطعه أن غوستاف يوهانس قد فارق الحياه.

He had not long survived his return, said his wife.

وقالت زوجته إنه لم يعس طويلا بعد عودته.

The doings at sea in 1925 had broken him.

لقد حطمته الأحداث التي وقعت فى البحر عام 1925.

He had told her no more than he had told the public.

لم يخبرها بأكثر مما أخبر به العامه.

But he had left a long manuscript of "technical matters".

لكنه ترك مخطوطه طويله بخصص "مسائل فيه."

These notes of the voyage had been written in English.

لقد كُتبت هذه الملاحظات الخاصه بالرحله باللغه الإنجليزيه.

Evidently in order to safeguard her from the peril of casual perusal.

من الواضح أن ذلك كان لحمايتها من خطر الاطلاع العابر.

He had gone for a walk through a narrow lane near the Gothenburg dock.

لقد ذهب فى نزهه عبر رفاق ضيق بالقرب من رصيف عوتبرع.

A bundle of papers falling from an attic window had knocked him down.

تسبب حزمه من الأوراق سقط من نافذه العليه فن سقوطه أرضاً.

Two Lascar sailors at once helped him to his feet.
قام بحاران من بحاره لاسكار بمساعدته على الوقوف على قدميه على الفور.

But before the ambulance could reach him he was dead.
لكن قبل أن تصل إليه سياره الإسعاف كان قد فارق الحياه.

The physicians found no adequate cause for his death.
لم يجد الاطباء سبباً كافياً لوفاته.

They mostly attributed his death to heart trouble.
وقد عزا معظمهم وفاته إلى مشاكل فن القلب.

But they added his weakened constitution most likely
contributed.
لكنهم أضافوا أن ضعف بيته الجسديه ساهم على الأرجح فن ذلك.

I now felt a deep gnawing at my vitals.
سعرت الآن بحر عميق فن أعصابن الحيويه.

A dark terror which will never leave me till I, too, am at rest.
رعب مظلم لن يفارقني حتى أرتاح أنا أيضاً.

Whether my death will come "accidentally" or not I can't tell.
لا أستطيع الجزم ما إذا كان موتي سيأتي "عن طريق الخطأ" أم لا.

I spoke to the widow about her husband's work.
تحدثت إلى الأرمله عن عمل زوجها.

And I persuaded her I had a "technical" connection to him.
وأقنعتها بأن لدى صله "تقنيه" به.

So she felt I was sufficiently entitled to the manuscript.
لذلك سعرت أني أستحق المخطوطه بشكل كافٍ.

And so I attained the dead man's writing.
وهكذا حصلت على كتابه الرجل الميت.

I began to read the documents on the boat to London.
بدأت بقراءه الوثائق على متن السفينه المتجهه إلى لندن.

They were little more than simple, rambling notes.
لم تكن سوى ملاحظات بسيطه ومتشعبه.

A naive sailor's effort at a post-facto diary.
محاوله ساذجه من بحار لكتابه مذكرات بعد وقوع الحدث.

He strove to recall that last awful voyage day by day.

سعى جاهداً لاسعاده ذكريات تلك الرحله المروعه الأخيره يوماً بعد يوم.

I cannot attempt to transcribe his notes verbatim.

لا أستطيع محاوله نسخ ملاحظاته حرفياً.

The manuscript is clouded with vagueness and redundance.

المخطوطه مليئه بالغموص والتكرار.

But I will tell the gist of what he wrote.

لكن سأذكر خلاصه ما كتبه.

Perhaps then you will understand why I stuffed my ears with cotton.

لعلكم ستفهمون حينها لماذا حشوت أذني بالقطن.

The sound of the water against the vessel's sides became unendurable.

أصبح صوت الماء وهو يرتطم بجوانب السفينه لا يطاق.

***

Johansen, thank God, did not quite know what he had seen.

لحسن الحظ، لم يكن يوهانس يعرف تماماً ما رآه.

But it is evident he had seen the city and the Thing.

لكن من الواضح أنه رأى المدينه والشيء.

I shall never sleep calmly again when I think of the horrors.

لن أنام بسلام مره أخرى عندما أفكر في الاهوال.

The horrors that lurk ceaselessly behind life in time and space.

الأهوال التي تتربص بلا هواده خلف الحياه في الزمان والمكان.

Those unhallowed blasphemies that come from elder stars.

تلك التجديفات المسمومه التي تصدر عن النجوم القديمه.

Dreamers beneath the sea known only by a nightmare cult.

حالمون تحت سطح البحر لا يعرفهم إلا طائفه من الكوابيس.

A cult ready and eager to release these monsters into the world.

طائفه مستعده ومسوقه لإطلاق هذه الوحوش في العالم.

Whenever another earthquake raises their monstrous stone city again.

كلما هز زلزال آخر مدينتهم الحجريه الضحمه من جديد.

When Cthulhu is under the light of the sun once more.

عندما يكون كاثولو تحت ضوء الشمس مره أخرى.

Johansen's voyage had begun just as he told it to the vice-admiralty.

بدأت رحله يوهانس تمامًا كما أخبر بها نائب الأميراليه.

The Emma, in ballast, had cleared Auckland on February 20th.

غادرت السفينه "إيما" ميناء أوكلاند فى 20 فبراير وهى محمله بالصابوره.

The ship had felt the full force of that earthquake-born tempest.

لقد شعرت السفينه بالقوه الكامله لتلك العاصفه الناجمه عن الزلزال.

The horrors from the sea-bottom that filled men's dreams.

الأهوال القادمه من قاع البحر والتى ملأت أحلام الرجال.

Once under control again the ship was making good progress.

وبمجرد استعاده السيطره، كانت السفينه تحرز تقدماً جيداً.

But then the ship was held up by the Alert on March 22nd.

لكن السفينه تأخرت بسبب الإنذار فى 22 مارس.

I could feel the mate's regret as he wrote of her bombardment and sinking.

شعرت بندم رفيقى وهو يكتب عن قصفها وغرقها.

Of the swarthy cult-fiends on the other boat he speaks with horror.

يتحدث برعب عن أتباع الطائفه ذوى البشره الداكنه على متن القارب الآخر.

There was some peculiarly abominable quality about them.

كان هناك سيء بغيض بسكل غريب فيهم.

Something made their destruction seem almost a duty.

سيء ما جعل تدميرهم يبدو وكأنه واجب.

This point was brought up during the proceedings of the court of inquiry.

وقد أعرب هذه النقطه حلال جلسات محكمه التحقيق.

Johansen shows ingenuous wonder at the accusation of ruthlessness.
يُظهر يوهانس دهسه بريئه إزاء اتهامه بالقسوه.

Curiosity is what drove the men on in their captured yacht.
كان الفصول هو ما دفع الرجال للمضي قدماً في يحتهم الذى تم الاستيلاء عليه.

Sticking out of the sea the men sighted a great stone pillar.
وبينما كان الرجال يبررون من البحر، لمحوا عموداً حجرياً ضحماً.

In South Latitude 47° 9', West Longitude 126° 43' they come upon a coastline.
عند حط عرض جوبي 47° 9'، وحط طول غربي 126° 43' يصلون إلى حط ساحلي.

The coastline was of mingled mud, ooze, and weedy Cyclopean masonry.
كان الحط الساحلي عباره عن مزيج من الطين والطمي والبناء الضحم المغطى بالأعساب.

Nothing less than the tangible substance of earth's supreme terror.
ليس أقل من الماده الملموسه لأقصى درجات الرعب على الأرض.

They had come across the nightmare corpse-city of R'lyeh.
لقد صادفوا مديته الجثت الكابوسيه رليه.

A city built in measureless eons behind history.
مديته بُنيت على مدى عصور لا تحصى حلف التاريخ.

Monuments to vast loathsome shapes that seeped down from the dark stars.
نصب تذكاريه لأسكال ضحمه بغيضه تسربت من النجوم المظلمه.

There lay great Cthulhu and his hordes for incalculable cycles.
هناك رقد كاثولو العظيم وجحافله لدورات لا تُحصى.

Hidden in green slimy vaults, they sent out their thoughts.
كانوا يرسلون أفكارهم محتبسين في أقبيه حضراء لزجه.

The thoughts that spread fear to the dreams of the sensitive.
الأفكار التي تنسر الحوف في أحلام الحساسين.

The thoughts that called imperiously to the faithful.

الأفكار التي نادت المومسين ببره أمره.

"Come on a pilgrimage of liberation and restoration."

"هيا بما في رحله حج للتحرر والاسعاده".

All this horror Johansen had no way of suspecting.

كل هدا الرعب لم يكن لدى يوهانس أي فكره عنه.

But God knows he had soon seen enough!

لكن الله يعلم أنه سرعان ما رأى ما يكمن!

I suppose what they saw was only a single mountain-top.

أطن أن ما رأوه لم يكن سوى قمه جبل واحده.

Soon the rest of the city emerged from the waters.

وسرعان ما طهرت بقيه المدينه من المياه.

The hideous monolith-crowned citadel where great Cthulhu
was buried.

القلعه البسعه المتوجه بالصخره الصخمه حيب دُفن كـولو العطيم.

I shudder to think of all that may be brooding down there.

أرتجف لمجرد التفكير في كل ما قد يكون كامناً هناك.

And I almost wish to kill myself to stop these thoughts.

وأتمنى تقريباً أن أقتل نفسي لاتوقف عن هده الافكار.

***

Johansen and his men were awed by the cosmic majesty.

أعجب يوهانس ورجاله بالعطمه الكونيه.

They beheld the sight of this dripping Babylon of elder
demons.

لقد ساهدوا مسهد بابل هده المبلله بالسياطين القديمه.

They must have guessed without guidance what it was they
saw.

لا بد أنهم حمسوا دون توجيه ما رأوه.

What they saw was nothing of this or of any sane planet.

ما رأوه لم يكن سيئاً من هدا الكوكب أو من أي كوكب عاقل.

The unbelievable size of the greenish stone blocks.

حجم كل الحجر الأخصر بسكل لا يصدق.

The dizzying height of the great carven monolith.
الارتفاع الساهق للصحره المحوته الصحمه.

And then there was the bas-reliefs found on the captured ship.
نم كانت هناك النقوس البارره التن عُثر عليها على السفيمه التن نم الاستيلاء عليها.

The colossal statues mirrored the scene on the carvings.
عكست النمائيل الصحمه المسهد الموجود على النقوس.

Johansen achieved something very close to futurism.
حقق يوهانس سيئاً قريباً جداً من المسهبليه.

Because he did not describe any definite structure or building.
لأنه لم يصف أئ هيكل أو مبنى محدد.

He dwelled on the broad impressions of vast angles and stone surfaces.
تأمل فن الانطباعات العامه للروايا الساسعه والأسطح الحجريه.

Surfaces too great to belong to anything right or proper for this earth.
أسطحّ أكبر من أن تنمن إلى أئ سئء صحيح أو مناسب لهذه الأرض.

Surfaces impious with horrible images and hieroglyphs.
أسطح نجسه نحمل صوراً مروعه ورموزاً هيروعليميه.

There is a reason I mention his talk about angles.
هناك سبب لذكرى حديثه عن الروايا.

It reminds me of something Wilcox had told me of his awful dreams.
يذكرنن ذلك بسئء أحبرنن به ويلكوكس عن أحلامه المروعه.

He had said that the geometry of the dream-place he saw was abnormal.
قال إن هندسه المكان الذئ رآه فن الحلم كانت عير طبيعيه.

Non-Euclidean spheres unlike anything here on earth.
كراب عير إقليديه لا مئيل لها على الارض.

Loathsomely redolent dimensions completely unlike ours.

أبعاد كريهة الرائحة نختلف تماماً عن أبعادنا.

Now a seaman was describing the exact same thing.
والآن، كان أحد البحاره يصف الشيء نفسه تماماً.

They bad both had the same terrible glimpse of this reality.
كلاهما كان لديه نفس النظره المروعه لهذا الواقع.

Johansen and his men landed at a sloping mud-bank.
نزل يوهانس ورجاله عند صفه طينيه منحدره.

And they looked up at this monstrous Acropolis.
ونظروا إلى هذه الاكروبوليس الضخمه.

They clambered slippery up over titan oozy blocks.
تسلقوا بصعوبه فوق كتل عملاقه لزجه.

Blocks which could have been no mortal staircase.
كتل لم يكن من الممكن أن تكون درجاً بشرياً.

The very sun of heaven seemed distorted in this mist.
بدت شمس السماء نفسها مشوهه في هذا الضباب.

A polarizing miasma welling out from this sea-soaked
perversion.
ضباب مُميز للاستقطاب ينبعث من هذا الانحراف المُشبع بالبحر.

Twisted menace and suspense lurked in those elusive rocks.
كانت تلك الصخور المراوغه تنطوي على تهديد ملتو وتشويق.

A second glance showed concavity where the first showed
convexity.
أظهرت نظره ثانيه التقعر حيث أظهرت النظره الأولى التحدب.

Something very like fright had come over all the explorers.
أصاب جميع المستكشفين شعور أشبه بالخوف.

Each man would have fled had he not feared the scorn of the
others.
كان كل رجل سيهرب لولا خوفه من ازدراء الآخرين.

And it was only half-heartedly that they vainly searched.
ولم يكن بحثهم إلا بفتور.

They were looking for some portable souvenir to bear away.
كانوا يبحثون عن تذكار محمول ليأخذوه معهم.

It was Rodriguez, the Portuguese, who climbed up the foot
of the monolith.

كان رودريعير البرنعالن هو من نسلق قاعده الصحره الصحمه.

From there he shouted of what he had found.

ومن هناك صرح بما وجده.

The rest followed him to the foot of the monolith.

وبعه الباقون إلى أسفل الصحره الصحمه.

They looked curiously at the immense door in front of them.

نطروا بمصول إلى الباب الصحم أمامهم.

The now familiar squid-dragon was carved on the door.

نم نمس سكل السين الحبارى المألوف الان على الباب.

It was, Johansen said, like a great barn-door.

قال يوهاسس: "كان الامر أسبه بباب حطيره كبير."

Although they said it only gave the impression of a door.

على الرعم من أبهم قالوا إنها نعطن انطباعا بوجود باب فمط.

They could not decide if the door lay flat like a trap-door.

لم يسطيعوا نحديد ما إذا كان الباب مسطحا مسل باب المصيده.

Or maybe the opening was slanted like an outside cellar-
door.

أو ربما كانب الفمحه مائله مسل باب قبو حارجن.

As Wilcox would have said, the geometry of the place was
all wrong.

وكما كان سيمول ويلكوكس، فإن هندسه المكان كانب حاطبه نماماً.

One could not be sure that the sea and the ground were
horizontal.

لا يمكن للمرء أن يكون مـأكداً من أن البحر والأرض أفميان.

Hence the relative position of everything else seemed
phantasmally variable.

وبالسالن، بدا الموقع السبن لكل سنء آحر منعيراً بسكل وهمن.

Briden pushed at the stone in several places, without result.

فام بريدن بدفع الحجر فن عده أماكن، دون جدوى.

Then Donovan felt delicately over around the edge of the
door.

ثم تحسس دونوفان برفق حافة الباب.

He climbed interminably along the grotesque stone molding.

تسلق بلا هواده على طول الرحارف الحجريه العريبه.

Although, if you could really call it climbing is debatable.

مع دلك، فإن إمكانيه تسميتها تسلقا أمر قابل للنقاس.

Perhaps the door was more horizontal than vertical.

ربما كان الباب أفقيا أكثر منه رأسيا.

And the men wondered how any door in the universe could be so vast.

وتساءل الرجال كيف يمكن لأئ باب فى الكون أن يكون بهذا الاتساع.

Then, very softly and slowly, something began to happen.

ثم، بهدوء سديد وببطء، بدأ سىء ما يحدت.

The acre-great panel began to give inward at the top.

بدأت اللوحه الصحمه بالانحناء إلى الداخل من الاعلى.

And they saw that the door had balanced itself.

ورأوا أن الباب قد استقام من تلقاء نفسه.

***

Donovan somehow propelled himself back along the jamb.

تمكن دونوفان بطريقه ما من دفع نفسه للحلف على طول عتبه الباب.

And everyone watched the queer recession of the monstrously carved portal.

وساهد الجميع التراجع الغريب للبوابه المحنوته بسكل وحسن.

In this fantasy of prismatic distortion it moved anomalously in a diagonal way.

فى هذا الحيال من التسوه المسورى، تحرك بسكل غير طبيعى بطريقه قطريه.

All the rules of matter and perspective seemed confused.

بدت جميع قواعد الماده والمطور مشوشه.

The aperture was black with a darkness almost material.

كانت الفتحه سوداء بظلام يكاد يكون ماديا.

That tenebrousness was indeed a positive quality.

ذلك الظلام بالفعل صفه إيجابيه.

The men were spared from seeing the inner walls.

لم تجنب الرجال رويه الجدران الداخليه.

The darkness burst forth like smoke from its eon-long imprisonment.

انفجر الظلام كالدخان من سجنه الذى دام دهراً.

The sun was visibly darkened by flapping membranous wings.

كانت الشمس مظلمه بسكل واضح بسبب رفرفه الأجنحه العسائيه.

And the shadow slunk away into the shrunken and gibbous sky.

وانزلق الظل بعيداً فى السماء المنكمسه والمحدبه.

The odor arising from the newly opened depths was intolerable.

كانت الرائحه المبعثه من الأعماق التى تم فتحها حديثاً لا تطاق.

The quick-eared Hawkins thought he heard a nasty, slopping sound.

ظن هوكينز، ذو السمع الحاد، أنه سمع صوتاً مزعجاً وفوضوياً.

His ears were confirmed when It lumbered slobberingly into sight.

تأكد من صحه ما سمعه عندما طهر ذلك السيء وهو يترنح ويسيل لعابه.

Its gelatinous green immensity groped through the black hall.

تسللت كتلها الخضراء الهلاميه الهائله عبر القاعه السوداء.

And Its ooze and smell squeezed through the angled door.

وتسربت سوائلها وروائحها عبر الباب المائل.

The Thing went into the tainted air of that poison city of madness.

انطلق الكائن إلى الهواء الملوث لتلك المدينه المسمومه المليئه بالجنون.

Poor Johansen's handwriting almost gave out when he wrote of this.

كاد خط يوهانسن المسكين أن يتلف عندما كتب عن هذا.

He thinks two men perished of pure fright in that accursed instant.

يعمد أن رجلين لقيا حتفهما من سده الخوف في تلك اللحظه المسوومه.

The Thing cannot be described with our language.

لا يمكن وصف هذا الشيء بلغتنا.

There are no words for such abysms of shrieking and immemorial lunacy.

لا توجد كلمات تصف مثل هذه الأعماق من الصراخ والجنون الذي لا يوصف.

Eldritch contradictions of all matter, force, and cosmic order.

تناقضات غريبه في كل الماده والقوه والنظام الكوني.

A mountain that walked and stumbled on the earth. God!

جبل سار وتعثر على الارض. يا إلهي!

No wonder that across the earth a great architect went mad.

لا عجب أن أصيب مهندس معماري عظيم بالجنون في مكان ما من العالم.

No wonder poor Wilcox raved with fever in that telepathic instant.

لا عجب أن ويلكوكس المسكين أصيب بالحمى في تلك اللحظه التخاطريه.

The green, sticky spawn of the stars, was walking the earth.

كان نسل النجوم الاخضر اللزج يسير على الارض.

The Thing of the idols had awaked to claim his own.

لقد استيقظ كائن الاصنام ليطالب بملكه.

The stars were aligned again, as was predicted.

اصطف النجوم مره أخرى، كما كان متوقعاً.

An age-old cult had failed in their duties.

لقد فشلت طائفه قديمه في أداء واجباتها.

And a band of innocent sailors fulfilled their role by accident.

وقامت مجموعه من البحاره الأبرياء بأداء دورهم عن طريق الصدفه.

After vigintillions of years great Cthulhu was loose again.

بعد مليارات السنين، عاد كثولو العظيم إلى الظهور.

And now great Cthulhu was ravening for delight.

والآن، كان كثولو العظيم يتوق بشده إلى المتعه.

Three men were swept up by the flabby claws before anybody turned.

تم الإمساك بثلاثه رجال بواسطه المخالب المترهله قبل أن يستدير أي شخص.

God rest them, if there be any rest in.the universe.
الله يرحمهم، إن كان هناك راحه فى الكون.

Let it be known that their names were Donovan, Guerrera and Angstrom.
وليعلم أن أسماءهم كانت دونوفان، وجيريرا، وأنجسروم.

Parker slipped as he was trying to make his escape.
انزلق باركر أثناء محاولته الهرب.

The other three were plunging frenziedly back to the boat.
أما الثلاثه الاخرون فكانوا يهرعون بجنون عائدين إلى القارب.

They ran over endless vistas.of green-crusted rock.
جابوا مناظر لا نهايه لها من الصخور المغطاه بقسره خضراء.

Johansen swears he was swallowed up by an angle of masonry.
يقسم يوهانس أنه ابتلعه راويه من البناء.

An angle which shouldn't have been there.
راويه ما كان ينبغى أن تكون موجوده.

An angle which was acute,.but behaved as if it were obtuse.
راويه حاده، لكنها تتصرف كما لو كانت منفرجه.

Only Briden and Johansen made it back to the boat.
لم يعد إلى القارب سوى بريدن وجوهانس.

The two men had a moment of good fortune.
حظى الرجلان بلحظه من الحظ السعيد.

The mountainous monstrosity flopped down on the slimy stones.
سقط ذلك الوحس الجبلى الضحم على الصخور اللزجه.

And the beast hesitated floundering at the edge of the water.
وتردد الوحس وهو يتخبط على حافه الماء.

The steam boat had not entirely.run out of hot coals.
لم ينفد الفحم الساخن تماماً من السفينه البحاريه.

Despite the departure of all men for the shore.
على الرغم من رحيل جميع الرجال إلى الشاطى.

Feverishly the two men rushed up and down between wheels.

ادفع الرجلان جيئه وذهاباً بين العجلات بحماس شديد.

It was the work of only a few moments to get the engine going.

لم يستغرق تسغيل المحرك سوى لحظات قليله.

Amidst the distorted horrors of that indescribable scene.

وسط أهوال ذلك المشهد المشوه التي لا توصف.

Slowly their boat began to churn the lethal waters beneath her.

بدأ قاربهم ببطء فى إناره المياه القاتله نحوه.

And they moved along the masonry of that charnel shore.

وتحركوا على طول جدران ذلك الشاطى المدمر.

That strange coastline that was not from this world.

ذلك الساحل الغريب الذى لم يكن من هذا العالم.

***

The titan Thing from the stars slavered and gibbered.

كان الكائن العملاق القادم من النجوم يسيل لعابه ويهدئ.

Like Polypheme cursing the fleeing ship of Odysseus.

مثل بوليفيموس وهو يلعن سفينه أوديسيوس الهاربه.

Then great Cthulhu slid greasily into the water.

ثم انزلق كاثولو العظيم إلى الماء وهو زلق.

Bolder and more daring than the storied Cyclops.

أكثر جرأه وشجاعه من سايكلوبس الاسطورى.

Cthulhu pursued them through the water with cosmic movement.

طاردهم كاثولو عبر الماء بحركه كونيه.

Briden looked back from the ship and started laughing shrilly.

نظر بريدن إلى الوراء من السفينه وبدأ يضحك بصوت عال.

From that moment Briden continued laughing at odd intervals.

وممد تلك اللحظه، استمر بريدن فى الضحك على فترات متقطعه.

But Johansen had not given up yet.

لكن يوهانس لم يستسلم بعد.

He knew his ship had no chance of outpacing the thing.

كان يعلم أن سفينه ليس لديها أى فرصه لتجاوز ذلك السىء.

So he resolved on taking a desperate chance.

لذلك قرر أن يغامر بمغامره ياسه.

He loaded the furnace and set the engine for full speed.

قام بتحميل الفرن وصبط المحرك على أقصى سرعه.

And then he ran lightning-like on deck and reversed the wheel.

ثم ركض بسرعه البرق على سطح السفينه وعكس اتجاه الدفه.

There was a mighty eddying and foaming in the noisome brine.

كان هناك دوامه قويه ورغوه كثيفه فى المحلول الملحى الكريه الرائحه.

The steam mounted higher and higher into the sky.

ارتفع البخار أكثر فأكثر فى السماء.

And the brave Norwegian reversed the course of the chase.

وقام النرويجى الشجاع بتغيير مسار المطارده.

Before him rose the unclean froth like the stern of a demon galleon.

ارتفع أمامه رغوه قذره تشبه مؤخره سفينه شيطانيه.

He drove his vessel head on against the pursuing jelly.

قاد سفينه مباشره نحو الهلام المطارد.

The awful squid-head came nearly up to the yacht's bowsprit.

اقترب رأس الحبار البشع من مقدمه اليخت.

But Johansen drove on relentlessly against the writhing feelers.

لكن جوهانس واصل القياده بلا هواده فى مواجهه الحواجز المتعرجه.

There was a bursting as of an exploding bladder.

كان هناك صوت انفجار يشبه صوت انفجار المثانه.

There was a slushy nastiness as of a cloven sunfish.

كانت هناك رائحه كريهه تشبه رائحه سمكه الشمس المشقوقه.

There was a stench as of a thousand opened graves.

كان هناك رائحه كريهه كرائحه ألف قبر مفتوح.

And there was a sound the chronicler did not put on paper.

وكان هناك صوت لم يدونه المؤرخ على الورق.

For an instant the ship was befouled by an acrid cloud.

للحظه، عطت سحابه لاذعه السفينه.

The green cloud blinded Johansen and the mad man.

أعمت السحابه الخضراء يوهانس والرجل المجنون.

And then there was only a venomous seething astern.

ثم لم يكن هناك سوى عصب عارم في الخلف.

But God in heaven! What the two men saw next;

لكن يا إلهي! ما رآه الرجلان بعد ذلك؛

The scattered plasticity of that nameless sky-spawn.

اللدونه المبائره لذلك الكائن السماوي المجهول.

The injured thing was nebulously recombining.

كان السيء المصاب يعيد تركيب نفسه بشكل غامض.

Soon Cthulhu would be back in its hateful original form.

وسرعان ما سيعود كاثولو إلى شكله الاصلي البغيض.

But their distance was widening with every second.

لكن المسافه بينهما كانت تتسع مع كل ثانيه.

The ship was gaining impetus from its mounting steam.

كانت السفينه تكسب قوه دفع من بخارها المتزايد.

And eventually the cursed city was over the horizon.

وفي النهايه، اختفت المدينه الملعونه وراء الافق.

***

He did not try to navigate after their lucky escape.

لم يحاول تحديد المسار بعد نجاتهم المحظوظه.

His reaction had taken something out of his soul.

لقد انتزع رد فعله سيئاً من روحه.

He spent his time brooding over the idol in the cabin.

أمضى وقته عارفاً فى التفكير والتأمل فى الصمت الموجود فى الكابينه.

He looked after the laughing maniac in the boat.
لقد اعتنى بالمجنون الضاحك فى القارب.

And he attended to a few matters such as food.
واهتم ببعض الأمور مثل الطعام.

Then came the storm of April 2nd.
ثم جاءت عاصفة الثانى من أبريل.

On that day clouds gathered over his consciousness.
فى ذلك اليوم، تجمعت الغيوم فوق وعيه.

There is a sense of pure and refined delirium.
هناك شعور بالهذيان النقى والمهذب.

Spectral whirling through liquid gulfs of infinity.
دوامه طيفيه عبر خلجان سائله لا متناهيه.

Dizzying rides through reeling universes on a comet's tail.
رحلات مدهله عبر عوالم متبدبه على ذيل مذنب.

Hysterical plunges from the pit to the moon.
قفزات هستيريه من الهاويه إلى القمر.

And he plunged back again from the moon to the pit.
ثم عاد من القمر إلى الهاويه.

A cachinnating chorus of the distorted, hilarious elder gods.
جوقه مرحه من الآلهة القديمه المشوهه والمضحكه.

And the green bat-winged mocking imps of Tartarus.
والشياطين الخضراء ذات الاجنحه الشبيهه بأجنحه الخفافيس الساخره فى
تارتاروس.

Out of that dream came rescue; the ship Vigilant.
من ذلك الحلم جاءت عمليه الإنقاذ؛ السفينه "فيجيلانت."

The vice-admiralty court and the streets of Dunedin.
محكمه نائب الاميراليه وشوارع مدينه دنيدن.

The long voyage back home to the old house by the Egeberg.
الرحله الطويله للعوده إلى المنزل القديم بجوار إيجبرغ.

He could not tell anyone of what he had seen.
لم يستطع أن يخبر أحداً بما رآه.

Had he told the truth they would have thought he had gone mad.

لو أنه قال الحقيقه لظنوا أنه قد جن.

So he secretly wrote of what he knew before death came.

لذلك كتب سراً عما كان يعرفه قبل أن يأتيه الموت.

"Death would be a boon if only it could blot out the memories."

"سيكون الموت نعمه لو كان بإمكانه محو الذكريات".

That was the document Johansen left behind.

كان تلك هي الوثيقه التي تركها يوهانس وراءه.

And now I have placed this document in the tin box.

والآن وضعت هذه الوثيقه في العلبه المعدنيه.

In the box is also the dream carved bas-relief.

يحوى الصندوق أيضاً على نفس بارز مسحوب على سكل حلم.

And I have included the papers of Professor Angell.

وقد أدرجت أوراق البروفيسور أنجيل.

With this box shall go this record of mine.

سيوضع هذا السجيل الخاص بي مع هذا الصندوق.

These notes have become a test of my own sanity.

أصبحت هذه الملاحظات بمثابه احتبار لسلامه عقلي.

But I hope my discoveries are never be pieced together again.

لكني آمل ألا يتم تجميع اكتسافاتي مره أخرى.

I have looked upon all that the universe has to hold of horror.

لقد نظرت إلى كل ما يحويه الكون من رعب.

But now even the skies of spring are darkness to me.

لكن الآن حتى سماء الربيع أصبحت مظلمه بالنسبه لي.

Even the flowers of summer are forever poison to me.

حتى أزهار الصيف أصبحت بالنسبه لي سماً دائماً.

But I do not think my life will be long.

لكني لا أعتقد أن حياتي ستطول.

As my uncle went, so shall my end come.

كما مات عمي، كذلك سكون نهايتي.

As poor Johansen went, so shall my time come.
كما رحل يوهانس المسكين، سيأتي دوري أيضاً.

I know too much, and the cult still lives.
أعرف الكثير، وما زالت الطائفة قائمة.

Cthulhu still lives, too, I can only suppose.
لا يسعني إلا أن أفترض أن كاثولو لا يزال موجودا أيضا.

I assume Cthulhu is again in that chasm of stone.
أفترض أن كاثولو موجود مره أخرى في تلك الهوه الحجريه.

The city which has shielded him since the sun was young.
المدينه التي حمته منذ فجر التاريخ.

I know his accursed city is sunken once more.
أعلم أن مدينته الملعونه قد غرقت مره أخرى.

The crew of the Vigilant sailed over the spot after the April storm.
أبحر طاقم سفينه "فيجيلانت" فوق الموقع بعد عاصفه أبريل.

But his ministers on earth still worship his return.
لكن ورراءه على الارض ما زالوا يعبدون عودته.

In lonely places they congregate around their idol.
في الأماكن الموحسه يجمعون حول صنمهم.

And they bellow and prance and slay in satanic ritual.
ويصرحون ويرقصون ويمثلون في طقوس سيطانيه.

He must have been trapped by the sinking of his black abyss.
لا بد أنه وقع في فح عرق هاويه سوداء.

Or else the world would by now be screaming with fright and frenzy.
وإلا لكان العالم الآن يصرح من الحوف والجبون.

Who knows how the end will come about?
من يدري كيف سكون النهايه؟

What has risen may sink, and what has sunk may rise.
ما ارتفع قد يغرق، وما غرق قد يرتفع.

Loathsomeness waits and dreams in the deep.

الكراهيه سطر ونحلم فى الأعماق.

And decay spreads over the tottering cities of men.
ويسر الحراب على مدن البسر المداعيه.

A time will come where that city rises out the sea again.
سيأتى وقت نهص فيه تلك المديه من البحر مره أحرى.

But I must not think about when that day will come!
لكن لا يجب أن أفكر فى مى سيأتى دلك اليوم!

I have one prayer if this manuscript outlives me.
لدى دعاء واحد إدا عاست هده المحطوطه بعد وفاتى.

I pray my executors put caution before audacity.
أدعو الله أن يصع مسعدو وصيبى الحدر فبل السهور.

I pray this manuscript meets no other eyes.
أدعو الله ألا نمع هده المحطوطه على أعين أحرى.

***

Found among the papers of the late Francis Wayland Thurston, of Boston.
عُر عليها صم أوراق الراحل فراسيس وايلاند نورسون، من بوسط.